Xenowealth
A Collection

Tobias S. Buckell

DEDICATION

For everyone who supported my Xenowealth stories and
asked for more…

CONTENTS

ACKNOWLEDGMENTS

This book wouldn't have been possible without the amazing support of everyone who backed the Kickstarter:

Mhairi Simpson, Eric Damon Walters, Jaime Moyer, Matt Forbeck, Mary Sue, Max Kaehn, Storium / Stephen Hood, Ken Moore, Stephen Blackmoore, Erachio, confluence, Zachary Conklin Wight, W. Aaron Waychoff, The Mad Hatter, joem, Paul Bulmer, Rob Fenton, Alex Baxter, Marc Beyer, Chuck Wendig, J.R. Murdock, William Pearson, Chuq Von Rospach, katre, Joe Morrison, Mary Agner, Mary Robinette Kowal, Patti Short, Angie Rush, Joris Meijer, D D, Joshua Bluestein, Tony C Smith, Michal Jakuszewski, Aubrey, Mur Lafferty, Rose Fox, Angus McIntyre, JRob, Anonymous, Simo Muinonen, Kristin Buxton, Alex Dugger, Ginger Stampley, Impossibilis, oliver, Adam Roberts, Julie Winningham, Arun Jiwa, Győző Both, Lena Strid, Martin Debes, Schleproque, Steve Lieber, Jeff Rutherford, Brad Bulger, Greg van Eekhout, Kevin Hemingway, Michael Lebowitz, Torben Bjerregaard, Tom Negrino, Pierre Gauthier, Niels Erik Knudsen, Dennis Kuczynski, Chad Orzel, Veronica Henry, Joel Finkle, Steven Saus, Rob Karp, Nick Bate, Bonnie Warford, Mike Jones, Chris Taylor, Tom Dillon, Jon Lundy, Esther Singer, sherdman, Brenda Cooper, Adam Danger Taco Rakunas, Josh Smith, Joanne Burrows, Dennis Sorensen, Joseph Charpak, David Bickerstaff, Kelly Smith, Philip Harris, Paul Duncanson, Chan Ka Chun Patrick, Hugh Staples, Ib Rasmussen, Free Moby, Richard Campbell, Adam Selby-Martin, Fran Friel, Scott Morrison, Joshua Rosenblum, Derek Freeman, Rob Slater, Robert Szarka, AJ Lewis, John Dinley, E Lear, Edward Greaves, Cliff Winnig, Komavary, Norayr Gurnagul, Ethan Byrd, Sam Brady, Alasdair Stuart, Conrad Rader, Sam Freilich, Bryan Larsen, Michael Berkey, Christopher Weuve, Chris Moseley, David Zurek, Michael Feldhusen, AMD Hamm, Jim Wilson, Bradley P. Beaulieu, Dave Borne, Cristina Alves, Chad Reichhold, Rob Holland, Christopher Green, Michael Squires, Seth Elgart, RevBob, Steven desJardins, Marc D. Long, Paul Weimer, Ashley Rayner, Benjamin Nash, Mlorenson, Jeff Hotchkiss, Ronnie J Darling, Christian Berntsen, Hanne Moa, Catherine Stevenson, Charles Meyer, e-sabbath, Evil Kitten, Peter Niblett, Aeonsim, Erin Cashier, Benet Devereux, Cuddly Tiger, Lawrence M. Schoen, Derrick Etheridge, DG, Samuel Erikson, Mignon Fogarty, Glennis LeBlanc, Leland Eaves, Chris, Anthony Pino-Valle, Roger Silverstein, Hal DeVore, Chris Ruttencutter, Jeff Wikstrom, Samanda Jeude, Jackie Wyse-Rhodes, Larry Lennhoff, thatraja, and Brenda Cobbs.

THE FISH MERCHANT

Li Hao-Chang, standing in front of a colorful array of fresh-caught fish, bargains with a Cantonese peasant over the price of yellow-tailed snapper. Where the Wharf tapers out, and the harbor is too shallow for the larger trawlers, the fish market thrives over a patch of old concrete and dirt.

The peasant finally offers enough yuan to satisfy Li.

"Xie xie," Li thanks the peasant, wrapping the fish up in old newspaper. The edge of the newspaper catches Li's eye.

Signals From Outer Space, it reads.

Li doesn't much care. All men can be awed by discovery, for Li there is selling fish. He has to make enough to pay rent, to eat, and to save. If he doesn't sell enough fish for rent, the local thugs come over to beat him up. If he doesn't make enough to eat, his wife goes hungry, and if he can't save, he'll never be able to leave Macau and the smell of fish that seems to taint his life.

The frenzied noise dips slightly near the stall. Li looks up from tossing ice on the fish to see what it is. A dark figure in a duster, moving through the fish stalls with a quiet confidence.

Pepper.

The man called Pepper stops and sniffs. Li knows the air he sniffs is alive with fish, and street sewer, and sweat. And something else. On the edge of all the sandpapery shark and still croaking grouper is the smell of fear.

Li Hao-Chang watches Pepper carefully. Li stands nervously behind his untreated plywood table glistening with fish juices, and

1

keeps his eyes averted.

Maybe the mercenary senses something, maybe his reflexes are keyed up beyond belief, a soup of tailored chemicals thudding through his bloodstreams. Maybe he is about to reach beneath the heavy folds of his dark gray oilskin duster and pull out a massive shotgun.

Pepper's steely gray eyes roll over the street and bore into Li Hao Chang.

"Afternoon, Hao-Chang."

His voice is as artificially gray as his eyes. All are carefully designed with respect in mind. Li knows Pepper sure as hell isn't here to buy grouper.

"Afternoon, Mr. Pepper."

Li is careful to keep conversation at a minimum. Pepper is usually not out in the street to chat.

Pepper looks around the surrounding stalls, his presence cutting though the babble of the crowd. The kaleidoscope of multi-racial faces washes past Li's table, their differences slight in comparison to Pepper's own contrasting strangeness. Rastafarian mercenaries do not seem to belong in any landscape, let alone Macau. His leather duster hangs low, the soft rain running off in rivulets and his half dreadlocks are tied back into a ponytail.

Li notices slight movement in the far distance, the crowd jostled by someone, and his ears catch the distant delayed puff of a silenced weapon. Pepper's body jerks sideways, and he crumples to the sidewalk. A peasant hurries past, ducking. The man who steps forward out of the crowd pockets his gun, then leans over. Li can hear the distinctive British lilt.

"Oy. He's down."

A silver armored Rolls Royce with tinted windows quickly parts the wave of panicked fish buyers. The rear doors open forward, and the mercenary is pulled across the cement, up into the car. The Brit has enough grafted muscle to have trouble getting into the Rolls.

Li looks down at spotted grouper and waits for the Rolls to leave. When he looks back up there is only an empty sidewalk in front of his table.

"Ni hao," he mutters to himself. The sidewalk is not entirely empty. A small disk lies near a puddle of thickening blood, already rust colored against the dirty cracked concrete of the wharf.

Li darts out to pick it up. Pepper haunts the wharf regularly. If Li does him a favor and saves the disk, then maybe Pepper will do him a favor.

The disk, covered in green symbols Li doesn't understand, makes a 'snick' sound as he picks it up. He looks down at his finger to see a point of blood, and thinks maybe he has cut his finger on a piece of glass.

Li Hao-Chang returns to his stall and puts the case into his purse. Maybe Pepper will pay him yuan for the case.

If Pepper returns, he thinks, dabbing at the cut with a piece of newspaper.

But Li has faith in Pepper. Pepper gives off a mystique of calculated invincibility. Pepper walks the Wharf, and the Wharf stays away from him. All the local gangs, no matter what color. Tan Italian, pale American, each learn Pepper's skills the hard way. They never try again.

Blacks are particularly nervous around him. Pepper is chocolate, with a white's gray eyes. He shows no ties to skin, he kills black as efficiently as white or any other shade. They call Pepper the black ghost.

The black ghost, because after every battle, no matter the injuries, Pepper comes back to life. How many back-up blood pumps are laced through his torso? How much artificial adrenaline is produced by small chemical factories in his stomach? Are his eyes really spliced hawk gene? Rumors trickle.

Li Hao-Chang has seen this scene before. Pepper will be back.

Li Hao-Chang gets home early and hands Mei two snappers.

"Yi qi chi fan ke yi ma?" He asks very formally of his wife, as if they were meeting for the first time. Mei smiles and curtseys.

"I would be honored to have dinner with you." She has rice already boiling in a wok; the fish can be chopped and sautéed, then mixed with rice. She is used to fish. Fish boiled, fried, baked, or cooked in any manner she can think of. Fish broth she gives to him in a thermos for lunch. And breaded fish they eat for breakfast before he leaves.

Li knows she hungers for a beef stir fry almost as much as he does, but they are saving the money for the trip. Out of Macau, and over to Manila, then to the United States of America. This is why they switch between Mandarin and English, practicing the new language with each other.

"Wo ai ni," he says softly, kissing her hair. She laughs and pulls away with the fish.

"Let me cook the fish, Li, then we can talk of love over rice."

Li smiles and pushes through the beads into the washroom.

"Pepper was at the fish market," he says, scrubbing away at the smell of fish vigorously. It doesn't work. The smell stays on despite the hard loamy soap. It reaches into clothes, into the sleeping pallet, and into the walls of the house.

He rinses his hands and comes back into the kitchen.

"Did he buy any fish?"

Li laughs and moves over to help Mei cook, expertly searing the strips of fish she hands him over the bubbling oil. The aroma is sweet with Mei's spices, but still familiar.

"No, I do not think Mr. Pepper likes fish. A British car came and took him away."

Mei swears to herself and chops at the head of the snapper, startling him. Mei doesn't like the British. Her family maintains the distrust, over Taiwan, over the Opium Wars, all history that to Li is many generations buried.

He gives Mei a long hug.

"The British will not hold him long."

"I wonder," she says, "why they took him away? He is a dangerous man."

"Maybe they have something they want from him. Pepper, he knows things."

Li can tell, though, that Mei does not wish to speak about Pepper anymore. So he changes the subject, while testing fish broth with a wooden spoon.

"It is good, as usual."

"Xie xie."

Li takes a rice bowl and spoons in fish and broth, clicking his chopsticks, a gift from Mei's brother. He always honors Ahn's memory at meals with them.

"More foreigner tourists today," she says through a mouthful of rice. "I got generous tips. A man from Texas. I told him our dream. He was very nice."

"That is good."

Li talks to his wife about weather, and the new docks being built. She tells him about the white tourists she guides around the city of Macau. They record everything on little cameras as she herds them around in little groups like sheep. She does not believe they ever actually see the city, they hide behind the small screen, and icons like 'zoom', and 'pan left'.

Li chuckles. His wife is quick minded.

After dinner he washes the bowls quickly and follows Mei to their pallet. Even after five years he still finds it amazing that she gave up Beijing for him.

He kisses her, then they lower down to the pallet.

When he pulls out the government condom he can see the sadness in her eyes. He knows she wishes for children, but they can not afford a child now. Not until they reach America.

"It is all for the better," he says, knowing that the sadness will pass quickly, and that Mei will become her cheerful self after a while.

"I know," she says, pulling him to her. "It doesn't make it any easier."

A tapping wakes Li. He blinks the sleep out of his eyes and stumbles through the dark. It is raining, and a dark figure stands at his door.

Li fights a wave of dizziness.

"Hao-Chang." Pepper's voice penetrates Li's befuddlement, and he snaps awake.

Li quickly begs his pardon, though he's not sure if he says it in Mandarin or English. He wonders what the mercenary is doing here.

Pepper's steel eyes blink.

"Qing jiang ying wen," he says slowly, as if unsure of himself. His Mandarin is usually impeccable, now he stumbles over the words as if they are unfamiliar.

"In English," Li nods. "I am sorry. Of course. I have something you dropped, a disk, on the pavement, earlier today."

Pepper nods. Li notices that Pepper is in bad shape; blood soaks the shirt underneath the leather duster.

"It has a tracker in it. I followed it here."

"I will get it for you." Li turns to go back in for his purse, but Pepper grabs his forearm. Li reflexively tries to pull away, fear spiking as he turns back, realizing the grip is unbreakable. Pepper pulls out a small needle, ignoring Li's wince as he slides the tip under the skin.

"The disk is important, and poisoned, to kill the one that steals from me. You were infected, when you touched it. Now you will be safe."

Pepper walks into Li's kitchen and carefully sits down on the bench, just as Mei comes in, wrapping herself in a robe. Li looks down at the tip of his finger, then closes the door.

"Wan shang hao," she says, greeting Pepper.

"Evening," he replies. "I apologize for waking you. I'm hurt very badly, and I don't have anywhere to spend the night."

Mei shoots Li a quick glance of enquiry, what is this dangerous man doing here? Li wonders himself, but he thinks of Pepper's Yuan and America, and he nods okay to her. She reluctantly turns her questioning glance to Pepper.

"I will get you a blanket."

Li grabs his purse and hands Pepper the small disk. Pepper pockets it, then takes the blanket Mei comes back and offers. Within a minute the gray eyes slide shut, and the man is asleep.

Mei quietly makes a pot of tea, and they sit and look at the massive black man asleep on their floor.

"Is he going to die?" Li wonders, amazed. His voice cracks

slightly. Mei shakes her head.

"He will not die. He is strong, he is built to handle and take these kinds of things." She would know such things. She once studied medicine at Beijing University. "He will probably be here a while," Mei continues.

"What would you have me say?" Li hisses. "No? And refuse him?"

Mei doesn't answer, she stares just past him, disapproving. Li sips his tea and calms himself. She knows that he is making the best of what he can in the situation for both of them.

Li leans forward and kisses her on the forehead.

"I must go to the fish market early," he says. "I am going back to bed."

Mei's warm body is snuggled alongside him. Li reluctantly pulls away and into the cold morning. Pepper is asleep on the kitchen floor, the blanket Mei gave him discolored with rust brown stains.

The rain still beats a tattoo against the side of the small apartment.

Li makes tea, sipping it quickly, then pauses to grab two large wicker baskets before he leaves for the docks. There, in the dim light of the morning he buys his fish from the back of a trawler. An eerie, silent, process. Li points with yuan clenched in his fist, then the men shovel fish into his baskets.

He carries the load of fish back to his stall, back straining against the weight.

Mei comes over to the fish stall at lunch with his thermos of fish broth.

"Forgetful," she teases him.

"Always."

She kisses him on the nose. Then she furrows her eyebrows.

"Our 'guest' still sleeps. I washed and changed his blankets. He is feverish now. I think it will break before tonight."

"Can I sell you a fish?" Li asks, holding a large squid out at her. "Very delicious." Mei pushes it away.

"Bu shi. I do not want your fish, vendor, now go and sell it to some other poor soul."

Mei turns and walks away down the rows of stalls, and Li watches his wife walk with pride. She is a beautiful woman, and he is a lucky man. In America, they will do well, he thinks.

There is fish to be sold, though.

Pepper's face is much paler than it should be, and covered in a fine sheen of sweat. Li is worried.

"Ni hao ma?" Mei asks him.

"I am fine," Li replies. "But what of him?"

"Pepper is sick. But he is getting better," Mei reassures him. "His body knows what is best for him. The Westerners have things in his body that are cleansing it, and fixing the damage."

Li remembers some of Mei's tales about Western medicine. Tiny machines that he could not see even if placed on a fingertip, can run through Pepper's body to find what is wrong, then fix it.

Pepper mumbles through his shivering.

Most of it Li does not understand. It is in English so heavily accented he cannot make it out. It is not English like everyone else speaks, it comes from the Caribbean. Li hears it in music played in restaurants near the waterfront. Li thinks he sometimes hears some of this strange accent when Pepper speaks to him at the Wharf, but not much. Pepper must suppress it, he decides.

He takes his bowl of rice and fish and heads over to their pallet to eat it.

After washing, Mei kisses him fiercely, but tonight it is Li who is thoughtful.

"I cannot," he says, "with another man under the same roof." The apartment is small, and he cannot forget the presence of the large mercenary.

Pepper is sitting on the bench in the morning, sipping tea, his jaw a chiseled line of thoughtfulness. Mei makes to batter fish for a breakfast as Li grabs his two wicker baskets, but Pepper holds up a hand.

"You stay here, today, Li," he says in that startling voice. "I need you."

Li looks down at his baskets.

"I must sell fish."

Pepper holds out a fistful of yuan. It covers a week of fish selling, and Li looks greedily down at it.

Pepper hands the yuan to Li.

"You need not sell fish today. Buy breakfast for us, something with lots of meat. I need the protein. But not fish." Pepper smiles a perfect set of teeth. "I have an errand for you to run. It is very important." He has the disk Li rescued earlier in his hand.

"What is it you need, Pepper?"

With the thick fold of cash in his hands, under the watchful eye of Mei, Pepper has Li's full attention.

Pepper tells Li to first go straight down past the wharf into town, to David Tsung.

With the wad of yuan in his pocket Li decides to first detour down a street lined with food stalls.

He stops in front of a small cart on wheels.

'Wok on wheels' emblazons the side of the cart, in both English and Chinese characters.

Li is not as interested in deciphering the unfamiliar English symbols; the scent of meat frying on oiled metal draws him in. He realizes his mouth is full of saliva. He hands over yuan for a small dish, greedily scooping meat and sauce into his mouth, relishing the taste of meat.

"Xie xie," he says, but the cook has already turned away from him to toss more strips into the wok to sizzle and dance.

Li watches the cook tease ingredients into the mixture for several seconds as he finishes his meal, then tosses the paper dish at a gutter and continues on.

David Tsung is an old man from Canton. He sells computers. Or at least, Li thinks so, as the windows of the small store show computers in fading old pictures. As Li steps in a bell dings. He closes his eyes to muster courage, and wishes he had never picked up the tiny disk. Even despite the promise of Pepper's yuan Li is scared.

"What do you want?" A sharp voice from behind the counter.

"Ni hao. I am here to buy a laptop, and a cellular modem."

David Tsung looks Li up and down slowly, squinting eyes scrutinizing the shabby clothes, dirty hands. The smell of fish has entered the store with Li. Li self-consciously rubs his hands against his trousers to try cleaning them.

Tsung abruptly cackles laughter.

"You have won the lottery, then?"

Li shakes his head.

"What money do you have?" Tsung asks. Li pulls the black info-disk out and sets it on the counter in front of Tsung.

"Pepper says you should know what to do with this."

David Tsung jumps slightly at the mention of the name 'Pepper'.

"Shi. But I told him I would think about it, I never have promised anything. It is dangerous."

Tsung thoughtfully picks the disk up, then drops it and swears. Li sees Tsung's finger drop a bead of blood, and assumes that Tsung is also now poisoned. Li is having trouble staying calm. His heart is running away from him, and nervous sweat beads his brow. The threat of death through poison is an ancient bargaining chip, Li knows. It is all that Pepper has armed him with. He hopes it is enough to force the old man to do Pepper's will.

But Pepper's words are in his head, walking him through. Li can still feel the pleasurable press of the yuan in his pocket against the side of his leg, and the beef in his stomach, so he speaks up.

"Pepper says not to be alarmed. The infection will take a day to develop. Only Pepper knows the antidote."

Tsung's voice rises in pitch as he continues swearing, but he looks scared.

"Pepper wants a laptop with cellular modem," Li repeats. "And he wants you to make safety copies of this info-disk." As Tsung steps back from the counter Li sees the shotgun strapped to his forearm, and his heart quickens.

I'm going to die, he thinks. The poison isn't enough of a threat. Maybe Tsung is going to kill me. Does he think I carry the antidote with me?

But Tsung beckons for Li to come through into the back with him.

"You Pepper's messenger, eh? How is Pepper. He okay?"

Li nods.

"Good. I'm glad." Li follows Tsung through the door, and they stand in a room filled with computers of all ages in various states of disassembly. Tsung hunts through several drawers before he pulls out a small laptop. "Here, here," he says. Li accepts the small notebook and stands waiting.

Tsung plugs the disk into another computer. He fiddles around with something on a screen, then smacks his lips as the drive begins whirring.

"I will make copies."

Li nods. Even if Tsung weren't, how would he know otherwise? So he stands and waits for the old man to finish and hand him the original plus a copy.

"The antidote?" Tsung asked.

"Pepper says it is in the mail for you. It will arrive in time."

The little old tech-man seems to deflate even further into himself. He holds up another disk in his clawed hands.

"You tell Pepper I have copies. I will send them out if I don't get an antidote. You understand. Tell him."

Li nods.

"You make sure you tell him to send me antidote."

On his way back Li stops at the 'wok on wheels' and orders several dishes of Iron Plate Beef. Rice will be waiting at home. The cook remembers him and smiles as he hands Li the covered paper dishes all in a bag with the logo emblazoned on the side.

He splashes through the early morning with a faint smile. The sweet aroma of stir fried beef mixed with kuomo mushrooms and bamboo shoots reaches his nose.

"Wo ai ni," Mei says the second he steps through the door. She hugs him fiercely, and he kisses her back.

"I love you too."

Pepper waits for the exchange to finish before he steps forward.

"Did you get everything?"

Li unshoulders the strap of the laptop case and hands it over. Pepper unzips it and sets in on the small table in the corner.

"I bet Tsung was pissed."

Li nods.

"He swore much." He catches Mei's glance out of the corner of his eye. She is looking at the bag in his hand. He gives it to her.

Mei breezes out of the kitchen with a paper dish into their sleeping room. Li knows she doesn't want to be seen greedily bolting the food down. He respects that. He can still taste the aroma on the edge of his tongue. He desires more. Instead he crosses his legs and sits with Pepper.

Pepper's bulk dwarfs him.

"You risked my life for this, what is it?" Li asks.

Pepper looks up at him and makes a sucking sound with his teeth.

"Man," he says in English, "you risked your own life, for the money I gave you." He smiles perfect white teeth again. "But I shouldn't be hard on you. Na." Li notices the strange lilt still in Pepper's English. "It is a great secret."

"Some secrets are better kept secret."

"Not this one." Pepper boots up the small laptop, and it makes squealing noises as it dials into an invisible network. "This secret is exactly the kind that shouldn't be kept."

"Tell me."

"You read much, Li? Do you read the newspapers you wrap your fish in?" Pepper looks up and around. "A few months ago satellites around the world received a message from somewhere outside of the solar system. Then it stopped. No one could decipher it, it didn't make any sense, but it was definitely artificial." Pepper's yellowed nails are dancing across the small keyboard.

Li waits as he plugs the disk into the laptop.

"Of course, everyone is curious. What sent it? Will there be more messages? That's what I am here for. My superiors tell me to keep my eyes open and ears to the ground." The English adage is unfamiliar to Li, but he guesses the meaning.

"You found things."

"Observatories on each major landmass across the world are receiving similar messages now." Pepper shifts on the seat and reaches for a dish of beef. He keeps talking through a full mouth. "North and South America, Africa, Europe, Australia...but Chinese officials denied they had any message. It took two weeks to find this damn version of the message, I got it through a scientist working at a deep-space observatory in Canton. And the message he received is different from all the others. The Chinese clocks show that this message is received first, and only in China. And the intervals in between the message are getting smaller. The other signals are merely repetitions to make sure the rest of the world is blanketed."

"I don't understand."

"Hao-Chang. Whatever it is, it will come here."

Pepper unplugs the case and slips it deep into the folds of his duster.

"Now, everyone in the Western Hemisphere has a copy of the Chinese message. Everyone is in on the great secret." The modem is quiet, the screen asks if the user if they would like to send another message. "And there it is. For what it's worth. Now maybe foreigners will quit harassing me."

Mei comes back into the room, discretely wiping at her chin. Li unconsciously moves closer to her.

Before he reaches her there is a polite knock on the door.

Li knows that he has no neighbors here, and he knows Mei has no family anywhere near the wharf. The fact trickles down through his mind with a cold shiver. Pepper looks up from the paper dish and puts it to his side.

He reaches deep into the duster.

The knock comes again.

Only this time the door is flung aside and a dim figure is in the room. Pepper rolls and fires something loud through his duster. Instinctively Li closes his eyes against the noise. He drops to the ground, and stays still.

He hears more clatter, the sounds ringing his ears. His heart thumps loud, and he prays for life.

Mei gasps and falls near him. As Li looks down at his hands

he sees blood. Pepper and the assailant are gone, chasing each other through the maze of small huts and apartments.

"Mei," he whispers. The only response is a short gasp, Li can hardly hear it. He gets to his knees and bends over his wife.

"Mei."

He sees her reaching for air, but not getting any. Instead of exhaling she coughs up blood. It runs down her cheek and into the dirt floor. Li cannot find words; he starts to gather her up in his arms, but she coughs again, the action racking her small body. He holds her there, in his arms, just above the dirt floor.

Her eyes are glazed, wandering around the room unfocused. Li puts his face before her. For a brief second her eyes seem to focus on him, then they are looking past him, and he can no longer feel the slight flutter of her heart.

"Mei."

Li allows her body to gently slip back onto the dirt floor. He weeps, his tears mixing with the stale rain-water dripping in through the bullet-holes in the roof.

He barely notices the gun battle outside cease, or Pepper silently returning. Pepper stands at the door for a minute, then carefully crawls into a corner.

Li stays kneeled over the body of his wife for several hours.

Pepper shakes Li's shoulder early in the morning. Pepper is pale, and the duster is once more soaked in blood. But he moves with quiet confidence.

"I am sorry about your wife," he says. "She was a good woman."

Li looks at the man uncomprehendingly.

"Good woman? Of course she good woman," he yells, his command of a whole second language breaking in the horror of the moment, tears flowing. *"What know you of sorrow you son of a bitch?"* He screams. He wants to attack Pepper for cursing him so. He wants to see Pepper dead on the floor with his wife. He wants his wife back. He wants what has been ripped from him. And he is drowning in an empty void.

"My superiors have what they want," Pepper continues haltingly. "I have to leave and go home." He opens his duster to expose chewed up skin. Underneath his flat stomach the glint of metal flashes. "I was given orders to leave as soon as possible."

Li squints his eyes against the early morning light streaming in through the half open door.

"Go home. Never come back."

He turns back away and shivers as a draught of cold air passes through the room.

"I just wanted to apologize…and give you this." Pepper steps forward and hands Li another thick wad of bills. It is enough to go to America. It is enough for Li to do anything. Li throws the money back at Pepper.

"Keep the blood money. I do not want it."

Pepper takes the money and sets it on the small table next to the laptop. He looks around the room one last time, shakes his head, wraps his duster back around him, then steps through the door, softly shutting it behind him.

Li sits still for another few minutes, then carefully kisses Mei's forehead and gets up, rubbing at red eyes.

Pepper leaves the laptop, with the small black disk sitting by it, behind.

Mei's grave is a small one dug by the Macau missionaries. Li is not sure what else to do, and the eager white missionaries are thrilled to preach the good news to an ignorant foreigner. Li ignores them, and sets an elaborate bunch of flowers next to the headstone.

Li isn't stupid. Something grand is happening. The message senders are closer now. He wonders if the Western scientists have gotten Pepper's data. Someday the messages will stop, and an alien craft will shake the sky, part the clouds, and land in Canton.

Pepper is no longer seen on the wharf docks. And Li no longer sells fish. He has enough money to live well in Macau for the rest of his life. Pepper's gift is generous.

On the deck of a large old ship that stinks of diesel fumes, Li leaves Macau. Another peasant on the deck, another hoping for a new life. He ignores the crates of loud fowl, the grubby smiling kid with the caged cricket, and the old lady who loudly farts on the bench across from him. He braces himself against the heavy sea, letting the salt blow away the fish smell, looking back at the distant shore.

Two weeks later, on the shore of a small beach in California, Li tosses a small black disk into the water, careful to not let it prick him, and then drops a single Hibiscus in after it.

Li has heard, earlier, that Western scientists are in Canton, the Chinese government finally admitting the existence of its message. Pepper's work is done.

And today in Canton, everyone repeats with wonder, the scientists looked upwards at the sky in wonder as a sleek shining alien craft slowed to a gentle stop between the massive radio dishes.

Maybe they will bring an order to the chaotic world, Li thinks, or change the world in other, fairer ways. He wants to meet the distant entities, and tell them how important his Mei was to their historic event. But for now...

"Farewell, Mei," Li says.

Then he turns to walk back up the beach, smiling at the children screeching and running through the cold surf.

MANUMISSION

T his morning, when you wake up and look at your rippled reflection in the basin of water near the concrete wall of your cell, you only have one true personal memory left. It can't be that your entire life is based off this one event, so you suspect they've left it with you to piss you off. To 'motivate' you. To make you one raging motherfucker.

It's a riff on the Countee Cullen poem. You're six, standing on the street holding the anonymous arm of your mom, and the other kid staring back at you flips you off and calls you nigger.

That's all they really left you with.

Sure there's other stuff, you're no vegetable. You can use money, eat, walk, tap the net, and know just about anything headlined over the last thirty years. But anything specific is faded, general, lost behind static and fuzzy feelings.

You empty the basin with a flourish and look around your cell.

The headache, the all-over itching, the scars crisscrossing your entire body, that gets to you too.

You've signed yourself away, the men in the black suits have explained back when you first arrived in this cell. They sat across from you on a sterile metal table. The document they slid toward your burnt smooth fingertips is legit.

So you listened to them, and nodded, and they got up to leave.

Oh yeah, one last thing, they had said.

Your name.

Pepper.

And your last name?

They just chuckled and closed the door.

Nine o'clock. Newport, Rhode Island. A forest of masts bobs slightly, boats cheerfully tied at their docks. You slide off the blue awning over the side entrance to a small bar and hit the slippery cobblestones to face a portly middle-aged accountant with slicked back wiry hair.

"Oh shit..." is all he has time to say.

Then slumps.

The small wires that knocked him out recoil back up into your wrists with a flick. You squat over the man, push his trousers up his hairy calf, and look at the tattoo on the back of his knee. He's ShinnCo property. Your eyes scan for forgery, defects, get in closer for a finer look, where every hair seems to be tree-sized.

All good. You blink your eyes until they return to normal, the thin extra membrane rolling back behind your eyelids.

His hands are clammy when you grab them. His breath reeks of alcohol. With a grunt you pull him up onto your shoulder and stagger toward a waiting car.

What, you wonder, has Mr. James Edward leaked to the Federalists? You really don't want, or need, to know.

Twelve hours later, five thousand closer to freedom, an old 6.35mm Astra Model Cub pistol tucked in the inner pocket of your oilskin duster, you're sitting in the lounge of an airship over several hundred feet of water, languorously easing your way toward the next stop, Eleytheria.

It's moored out in the Atlantic off the Eastern Seaboard this month.

At street level the Gulf Stream winds kick through the downtown buildings of Eleytheria. Your oilskin duster takes on a life of its own, bucking, trying to pull you off course as you make the usual staggered path, random jigs, sudden stops in front of reflective surfaces. It's not even a conscious thing, checking for tails.

Monotone pedestrians in business camouflage, the grays and blacks of their seemingly timeless and conservative professions, mill past you.

It isn't New York, but any of them could have been plucked out and placed in that environment without even noticing. No, just a few miles away the salt clears the breakwalls in clouds of mist and hovers into downtown.

Eleytheria is a giant bowl riding the large open ocean. Free to go where it pleases. Do what it pleases.

Many things start in Eleytheria.

Like yourself, years ago, deep in the bowels of one of Eleytheria's denizen companies. You've found old archived public camera pictures of yourself walking down the streets, into the center of ShinnCo, to sign your self, this self, into what you know now.

Sometimes you hate your old self for selling you into this bondage. You wonder what he got? Lots of money? Some last great fling? Or were you just desperate, a wandering piece of hardware abandoned by some former First World secret gov project made obsolete by the Pacification?

You'd like to think you did it for some great cause, like helping your family out of a dire situation. But late at night you doubt it and think there was some stupid, selfish reason for doing it.

They'll never tell you. Because if it was something like a

family, you might try to contact them.

No. They have your memories. You'll get them back when you serve your contract.

It always comes back to Eleytheria. When your feet hit the seacreate, your nose fills with misted salt, and you have returned to the only home you know. All your recent memories, everything that is you, starts here. Ever since you woke up behind a garbage dump in the back alley of ShinnCo.

And they've never let you back in through the front doors because they know full well what kind of monster they created. They control you, but they don't sleep well at night. If you were to ever get near a door the automated security would hit you with an EMP pulse that would pretty much liquefy the machines in you, then the guns would reduce you to bloodied ribbons of flesh.

You won't be getting your memories back using the new skills they've grafted into you. No way. And they still have one final trick, to keep you close, to control you.

So you stand in front of a small food cart. A faded orange umbrella hangs limply over it. When you palm the metal rail, the countdown inside you resets. You're allowed to live for another week. A pointed way of letting you know you're motherfucking owned, and you don't get to stray. At all.

The edges of the umbrella flutter in the cold breeze, and on the other side of the cart an old Greek stands up.

"Morning Kouroupas."

"Morning, Pepper," he says, looking you up and down. "The usual?"

"The usual."

The front of the cart has a faded poster of a model with a strained smile, flat white teeth, holding up a gyro in perfectly manicured hands. They're 'heeeeros' she says.

"Lettuces, mayonnaises..." Kouroupas' crazy white hair flies all over the place in the wind. It makes him look like a mad scientist.

He slaps the flatbread down. A cloud of flour tickles your

nose.

A few browned strips of meat, some folded metallic paper, and you have your gyro, along with a small napkin neatly slid between your fingers.

You look at it, your eyes adjusting to the fibers, mapping out a pattern along the embroidered edges, translating the woven picture into words.

Susan Stamm. Ten thousand. Location. Eleytheria.

Ten thousand closer to getting yourself back. To freedom. And she's right here.

You fold the napkin and its encrypted directions into your pocket, pick up the gyro. Kouroupas smiles.

"Good day," he tells you. "Be careful."

You nod and slide a few bills over to him.

"You too."

Be careful. It's the first time Kouroupas seems to acknowledge that this isn't just a gyro purchase. Seems to be telling you something's not quite normal this time.

Out of sight of the gyro stand you toss the gyro into a trashcan that thanks you and trundles away.

Not nearly enough raw sugars in gyros for you. Takes too long to metabolize. What you need now is something to spike your blood sugar to combat levels.

Susan Stamm has done many, many unique things to hide her presence. But she's on the run and wants off the planet. To do that she has to come to Eleytheria. Once an hour, every hour, a capsule is launched into low Earth orbit.

To really get far away, Stamm has to get Out There from Down Here.

So you sit and flip through pictures of embarkees who've been photographed at all three entrance points. One by fucking one. And these are just the ones the Port Authority computers have served up as possible matches. ShinnCo is being very generous with info and resources right now. They really want her back.

You're sitting in a small outdoor café, eyes closed. On the right eyeball is Susan Stamm's corp ID photo. On your left is some random face pic snapped by the Port Authority entrance machine.

Then another random face.

You reach for the sugary soda, take a long cold sip, and the next picture comes up.

Another sip of sugar water. Gotta keep the machines inside you running happy.

You flip to another pic.

Ha.

She looks thinner than the last official photo. She's still five-nine, but now has a recently bobbed haircut and green eyes.

Four hours later you're in the lobby of a smaller Eleytheria hotel, looking up at the atrium eighty stories above you, licking the icing off a Danish. In the background, over the hum of people, over the echoing shouts of kids screaming and waving from several floors above, comes the explosive whip-crack of a capsule being thrown into space.

There was this mugger that jumped you a year ago. Before you even realized it you'd spun, broke both his arms and a leg, and the man lay in an unconscious heap by the side of a brick facade.

His clothes were ragged, he was thin, and when you held his gun in your hand, you realized that it was unloaded.

Ballsy. And pathetic.

By going through his wallet you found out that his name was Jack Connely. He

had three kids and a very attractive blonde wife. Jack had been a spacer entrepreneur of some sort, reduced to Earth living after the Pacification.

Now all the businesses could buy a ride into space. Move their offices up into alien stations, use alien services, buy alien products, machines. Not much use for small guys, you could hardly scrape together the price. But multinationals can, and now that they're all in orbit, or beyond, the pretense of even caring about the world they originated from was thrown out.

You could have used the money you found in his pocket, his day's take, though you couldn't use it toward paying off your ShinnCo contract. They only accept their own in house credit.

You couldn't even use the money to disable the shit laced all through your body. You tried that once before. Almost killed you on the table.

Instead, you sent his wallet and the money back in the mail to his family. And you added some of your own.

You're a good person, you tell yourself.

But it's very hard to believe when it was so easy, so automatic, to have grabbed that man's gun and pull the trigger, right down to within a hairtrigger of firing, before stopping.

That can't be all wired into you, right?

Susan Stamm walks through the revolving door, past a doorman, and on toward a cab. You shake your shoulders and arms, loosening up the great mass of coat around you, and step in behind her. She's better looking in person, unlike some of the dolled-up, make-up-caked women you've seen in the past.

As she grabs the gullwing door of the bubbly autocab she spots your reflection in the window and turns around.

"Could we share this ride?" you say. Already you flex the muscles in your wrists, begin to raise your left arm and coat to obscure her body. She'll fall, and you'll sweep her up and into the autocab with you.

As the autocab rides off you'll look like two lovers cuddling in the back.

Instead her eyes widen, hands curl into fists, and a small dart burrows into your stomach.

You're on the ground, convulsing. Spit flecks your lips. You break into a heavy sweat. Vomit tastes like sugar water, flowing out onto the concrete sidewalk. It takes effort just to slowly roll over.

The doorman turns around.

He moves, a blur that you know isn't natural, and hits Stamm from the side. She hits the door of the autocab, shattering the Plexiglas, and the doorman grabs her neck, turning her head to confirm her ShinnCo tattoo.

Small silver fans protrude from the back of the man's neck. Antenna. You can see heat rising off his uniform, rippling the air around him. A timeshare. Not under his own control then--just renting his body for sudden on-the-spot jobs like this one.

You have a choice. Give it up. Let this competitor grab her, kill her, whatever.

Or.

With just a quick flex of your arms the wires spit out of your wrists and hit the back of his neck. The man spasms, lightning sparking across the surface of his skin. The antenna melt, dripping down the back of his collar. He spins around and raises his arms.

"Oh fuck," he screams, the link to whatever controls him from orbit gone. "I'm burning. They killed me! I'm burning!"

As he staggers toward the door, people gather. Someone tries to get the doorman to sit down. Someone 911s to call this in, speaking into his pinkie finger.

On your hands and knees, eyes burning and streaming tears, wires retracted back into your wrists, you push forward into the car. You grab Stamm, pull her in with you, and barely manage to shut the door.

She's in better shape than you, coming back to consciousness as you vomit sugar water all over her red high heels.

"Drive, damnit," she shouts at the cab's autopilot, and gives an address.

"Damage has been detected," it warbles. "Failure mode initiated. A replacement cab is on its way. We apologize for the delay."

"Shit."

The cab rocks as she leans forward.

Your muscles fail.

Your brain goes zero.

You're out.

There are rooms and then there are rooms. They're square more often than not, with white walls. But this one has dirty laundry, fake wooden paneling, a giant mirror on a wall, and a small cot that you're lying on.

A wicker chair next to you creaks. Soft hands stroke your

forehead.

"You're tough. That was supposed to kill you."

"I feel like shit." Every pore hurts.

"I would imagine." A finger traces the scars all over your body. "I'm sorry. I think I may have got the wrong person. It was the doorman I should have shot, he was the one coming for me. Who are you?"

Don't say anything.

Just shiver and turn back off. It's easier.

You wake up hungry and naked. Disoriented. You have no internal time. The small set of numbers that usually hover in the corner of your left eye is gone.

There's a pink bathrobe on the wicker chair that you grab as you sit up.

It takes everything you have to stand. Muscles protest, and every cell seems to ache.

"Feeling better?"

She's sitting by the kitchen counter, hands up, watching you warily.

You nod.

"Okay. So here are the rules. Any sudden moves I fire another one of these pips into you. If your hands aren't where I can see them, I shoot. I doubt you survive another one. So sit. Put your hands on your lap."

The bathrobe is comfortable. You slowly wrap it tighter around you and sit. Her tone drips with suspicion, guarded overtones. The air is tense.

She points at your leg. That's where they tattooed the small logo on you. Inner thigh. It really, really hurt.

"You're ShinnCo."

"Yes." She knows, you know. No point in denying.

"And the doorman?" she asks. "Did you know about him

ahead of time?"

You shrug.

She stares at you and you stare right back, not sure where this is going. You have the faintest sense that you'll get out of the door alive.

"Why are you still here?" you ask, which also implies, why am I still alive? "You could have left me here."

Stamm smiles.

"I felt bad for you."

That is not the response you really expected. And you don't believe it for a second. Someone this dangerous isn't that stupid.

"You know what I am..."

"Get real. They want me alive. You're not that dangerous. Neither was the doorman, he was just a backup. It's unfortunate they don't care a whit about his life."

You've never spotted backups of any sort before. This is different. Very different. She spots the frown.

"Is this your first high profile recapture?" Off in the distance is the whipcrack of another space launch, and she smiles. It's a broad one, full of glee. "Look, I'm within walking distance of getting away. They're getting desperate. I shouldn't have gotten this far. You're a backup, the doorman was an emergency backup, and the first three they sent after me are all lying in alleys somewhere."

She's dangerous.

Kouroupas tried to warn you.

"So what now?" you ask.

"Well I'm hungry and making some breakfast. Can I get you anything?"

You smile.

"Anything with sugar, I could really use something sweet."

She nods.

"Yeah, I'll bet you could, but I know what makes you tick." Your smile drops. "None of that for you. I'm leaving you weak, and slow for now. Just stay on the bed, don't move, and I'll bring you some diet soda."

You stare at her, and she laughs at you.

"I know a lot about those systems in you. How do you think I ended up with those little pips I hit you with? I designed them myself."

She walks into the kitchen, opens the fridge, and tosses you a can.

"Drink up...what is your name?"

You look down at the sugarless drink in your hands.

"Pepper," you say.

Susan Stamm. ShinnCo property since birth. Mother died having her, orphanage signed Susan over. She starts telling you all this stuff as she sits at a small table across from you and eats obscene amounts of breakfast sausage and eggs. The place reeks of it.

"You never even realize there is a different way of life," Susan says. "But I remember, when I was twelve, suddenly understanding that there were people who didn't have have logos on their bodies, who didn't have to report into minders once a day, who weren't being encouraged to study certain things that the company needed." She picks up a greasy link, pauses. "And then I decided I would escape it."

"How many years has that been?"

She flashes a smile and downs the sausage.

Then the dishes are tossed in the sink, she washes her hands while looking over her shoulder at you. You're still sitting in the pink bathrobe, sipping from the can.

"Just on the other side of Eleytheria is a launcher. I have a ticket off this world, and out there I have passage far out as crew on a mining ship. I know it won't be easier, but I'll be my own person." She raises a wrist. "I can burn this fucking logo off my skin."

"So you'll leave me here?"

She shakes her head.

"I have a proposition. You can't buy your freedom from ShinnCo, I'll bet, not for a long time yet. But what would you do for a ticket offworld?"

You just stare at her.

She takes it as hesitation.

"You owe me your life anyway. I need someone at my back, because if it's just me they'll try and pick me up at the gates to the launcher. Last ditch, overwhelming numbers."

"Okay." Opportunity glints in your eyes. At any point along this journey you may have an opportunity to overpower her. She spots the reaction. She thinks she has you.

"You'll walk me to the launcher, then I'll hand over the ticket. Try to double cross me before then and I'll fire another one of these nasty little critters into you. So it's in your best interests to work with me."

You nod.

She laughs.

"You realize you're free, don't you? You weren't just physically disabled," she says. "I scrubbed clean all your systems. You understand what that means?"

You test everything she has just said, and she is right. But...

When you look down to your wrists she steps back slightly. It's an unconscious move.

"Those still work," she says. "They're bio-mechanical. Nothing that can be scrambled, infected, or shut down."

For the briefest flash of a moment you've seen freedom. And then, you think to yourself, there is the matter of the countdown. That's firewalled off from the rest of your body and bio-mech. You can't see the countdown, but you know it's there. You don't explain this to her. Right now she thinks you're in her debt.

Play along.

"I've set you free from them," she says. "You can do anything you want now."

You nod again. "Okay, fair enough. I'll help you for the ticket.

Can I have my clothes back?"

The smile on her lips fades. She sizes you up, squinting. Apparently something satisfies her.

"Other side of the bed."

They've been washed, pressed, and folded into a neat pile. The Astra Model Cub pistol lies on top of them all. It's loaded.

Golden. Like that tantalizing glimpse of freedom she'd tried to give you.

Fifteen minutes later you're both out the door. You've got the overcoat draped over your right arm. You're weak, tired, and at a disadvantage, but all it will take is one well-placed shot where you can drop behind some cover, and she's down.

Susan faces you as she locks the door, still wary, but there is joy in her face. She can see the end of the road.

It's almost sad.

You walk down a corridor toward a pair of steel doors. As sunlight spills into the dimly lit area, you scope a vending niche just ahead and to the right. A drink machine hums a long low note. All you have to do is slow down, just get behind her by one step, shoot her, and use the machine for cover if she tries to use one of those lethal darts.

Two shadows force their way through the doors at the end of the corridor.

The gun's easy enough to spot; you duck and jump to your side. Susan fires at one of them as you dodge into the niche.

What puzzles you is the wrenching pain in your shoulder that drops you to the floor in front of the neon glow of the soda machine.

They're not aiming at Susan.

That was meant for you.

Your chest is wet with blood and your left arm can hardly move, but with your right you feel around the inside of your

30

overcoat as Susan falls to the ground. Unconscious, not dead.

You drape the coat over the good arm to hide the Astra and wait.

It's Kouroupas that turns the corner. His wild hair makes a halo around his head, bathed and filtered in the light of a flickering fluorescent overhead. There is no waiting, he looks down at the overcoat hanging over your right arm, hesitates for a second, and you fire four times in a row, blowing a hole in the overcoat that the muzzle sticks through.

"Damn it." Kouropas looks shocked as he slumps to the ground.

You crawl over to him and lean close.

There are no last words, no apologies or explanations, just his creased eyes looking up at the ceiling, his flour covered hands holding his bloody stomach, and then he stops breathing.

With some effort you retrieve his gun, pocket it with your Astra, and slump with your back against the soda machine.

Fifteen sodas later you shake Susan awake again. The first time you tried, after plucking the feathered dart out of her neck, she just lolled back into unconsciousness.

Your shoulder is packed with a shirt torn off the anonymous, dead, would-be assassin at the far end of the corner. You're still seeping blood.

"Come on," you whisper to her. "You need to wake up."

Her eyes snap open.

"No!" she shouts, throwing her hands up in front of her. You grab her wrists, a quick snapping motion, and look at her. She thinks she's been captured and been taken back to ShinnCo.

"You're okay, you're still here in the lobby. You got one of them first, I got the other."

She looks at you, then calms.

You're keyed up, your body's retooling itself, parts coming

back online. She'd given you an out, a way to leave. Your body, deactivated, could have been worked over by any shitty street surgeon. There was the slightest chance you could have found a way to be free eventually, thanks to her trick.

Now the insulin is surging, the blood sugar's up, and the teenies in your blood scurry around, revived and back to business.

You're back. Rebooted. Tiny emergency warnings flash in your vision, detailing the damage done to your shoulder. It numbs itself and the bleeding clots and stops.

Susan hardly protests as you pick her up off the ground by her wrists with one arm.

"Do you still have time to make your launch?"

She's dazed, but focuses.

"Yeah. Yeah. We need to move."

Gun in hand, the other shoved in a pocket so you don't move it, you sweep the area ahead. Nothing stops the two of you.

In the cab she asks you why you stayed with her.

You sit there, adjusting the bloodied shoulder bandage, and avoid her gaze.

"They came at me first," you explain. "I'm a target now." ShinnCo has spent too much time up in orbit, not enough time on the ground. You are just ants, resources to be used. And in their eyes you've turned on them, bitten them. It's easier to eliminate you and find a new worker of your talents than risk something going bad. You've seen it before. No doubt you'll see it again. "What good is bringing you in if they're going to shoot me as I try do it?"

"You could still have just left me there."

True.

You wrap your coat back around you and look up at her. "I owed you one."

The cab bumbles on down the road while you both sit in silence for a while. Then she puts a hand on your knee.

"You rebooted. I can fix you again, so you're free of all their machines."

You look down at her hand.

"Take too long. You have a launch."

"Yeah." She pulls back away, crosses her arms over her chest, and looks out the window. "I'm sorry."

"Don't be," you say. "Your trick probably wouldn't have worked anyway." And you tell her about the ticking bomb in you, the nano flechettes timed to go off unless they get their little code from that contact on the gyro stand.

We own you motherfucker.

"They aimed at me first," you tell her. Kouroupas came to finish it, and they'll get to aim at you again when you have to go back there to the cart in three days. Or you'll be sitting, standing, somewhere, when the bomb goes off. You'll look normal for a while, to bystanders, until your body falls down in a shapeless mass. Shredded from the inside out.

"That's why I rebooted."

You look out the window now as well, watching the terminals approach.

There isn't much to say after that.

There are some things you know about memory technology.

One is that it began here on Earth. Using existing technology: superconducting quantum interferometer devices that map specific memory recalls. It was pretty much there when the Pacification happened. With alien technology brought down out of orbit it got nudged along just a little further into maturity.

Two. The memories are burned out of your head. They aren't coming back.

Three. The same alien technology that matured memory alteration allows backups.

Four. When you figure out how to disable the bomb inside

you, you will then go out and find that backup.

If there is no backup, there will be payback.

You walk Susan up to the terminal booth. Several streets behind lie the bodies of more dead ShinnCo who tried to stop you. You stand on neutral ground. Even ShinnCo wouldn't piss off the alien launch corporation that owns Eleytheria. Overhead the floors sweep out over the road like wings. The architecture is impossible, like Frank Lloyd Wright on crack. The supports are too small. The wings too large. It's a building designed by something that evolved on a lower gravity world and is forcing their sensibilities onto an Earth object.

The inside of the booth is filled with a light pink gas of some sort. It's more than bulletproof; any hostile action you could take would result in vaporization.

Alien ticket takers don't put up with shit. Too many Earth terrorists tried to take out their aggression on them in retaliation for the Pacification. The orbital corporations that own the rest of the solar system found it annoying, so they put in countermeasures.

Susan scans her ticket in.

Inside the booth, tentacles move. Half of them are plugged into the wall, the other half seem to support a globular mass. This creature looks like a cyborg octopus. It's light years from home, trying to scrape out a living in a weird world, looking out at you with three eyes at the center of its trunk and burbling something.

"Clear. Proceed," the speaker orders.

The security gate to the right of the booth slides aside.

Susan turns to you. She slides an extra ticket into the palm of your hand.

"In case it ever works out..." she says.

You wonder if the memory of her walking through the security gate, or the memory of her hand sliding away from yours, could easily be burned out of your head.

Not this time at least.

Several minutes later the capsule thunders out in the great above and the thing in the booth hisses at you, wondering what your deal is.

Time to move on.

You stop at a public access point near the corner of a road.

The demands you send the ShinnCo emergency contact points are as follows:

One negotiator familiar with your case, with authority to bargain. The cart, fully functional, in the usual space. And you'll confirm the cart from a distance, making sure it isn't a fake.

Two hours. They couldn't get an identical fake, with heat generating machinery of the same signature inside in that time.

Or else?

Or else you have time enough to go hunting before the countdown hits the last second.

You'll need a hatchet, for starters.

It's a metaphorical high noon. They're not going to back off, and neither are you. The first sign of weakness is death. You're locked in, no turning back.

They set a nice trap. The gyro stand is up, and what looks to be a middle-aged man stands there. He isn't putting much into the facade, half-heartedly telling interested passersby that he's out of flatbread.

You spot the three snipers on balconies above.

Two men in doors nearby, lounging.

Four pedestrians.

One by one would take far too long, so you steal a bubble cab.

Even the new gyro guy doesn't spot you until you swerve the stolen machine off the road and slam into the cart. Flour, flatbread, meat, and sauces explode into the air. They drip off the door as you swing it up and open, using it for cover as you knock the stunned man out with a flick of your wrist, and pull him into the car.

The shots start. Silent insect-like buzzes and then explosions of concrete. The glass windows of the cab explode, the seats kick up leather and stuffing. In addition to the glass splinters buried in your face, the concrete shards ripping your overcoat apart, they hit you in the thigh, and then again in a foot.

Keep moving.

You grab the hatchet and smash the cart apart while keeping low, and pull out what you need. Your forearm gets hit, bone splitting out of the skin and causing waves of pain and nausea until things inside your body decide the pain is getting in the way of your ability to function.

The cab can barely hold everything. Glass bites you in the ass as you sit down and barrel out of there.

Engine smoking, tires flopping, it lasts long enough to get you deep into an alley.

The gyro man is coughing blood and dying in the back thanks to a well-aimed shot to the stomach. What you really want to do is get to work on him, make him forget about that pain and worry about a whole new universe of hurt. Maybe it will help you forget about yours.

Instead you work on bandaging your own wounds with strips of fabric torn off the overcoat and watch him struggle to stay conscious.

His eyes dilate, mouth drops open.

"I know about your memories," he croaks.

"You the negotiator?" You hadn't expected them to actually put him next to the cart. He ignores that, moves on.

"You don't have any. You never had any," he says quickly. "You came to ShinnCo looking for ways to reverse the process. But you were state of the art. Recent government surplus, useless after the Pacification. If ShinnCo didn't claim you, some other corporation would. So they screwed you over."

"I can't help you," you say. Even if an ambulance got here in time he wouldn't make it back.

The man closes his eyes and groans. The inside of the cab smells of shit from his ruptured stomach. His messy hands are both folded over, he's almost fetal.

"Fuck them," he rasps. "They told me this would be easy. That you wouldn't even get to cross the street."

"They fucked you. They fuck everyone."

You watch him.

"At least you're as fucked as me," he says, eyes still closed. It's almost a whisper now.

You don't bother to tell him the truth.

Another long moment passes.

"They have what you did know on a recording. You had something stored. They have that."

"And do you know what I was?" you ask.

He shakes his head.

Then shudders.

Passes out.

The actual dying will take a while more. You slowly shift, reach to his head, and snap his neck. After rummaging around you pull his wallet out. A picture of a redhead. Girlfriend? Must be, you think. No ring.

So what price are you willing to pay for your self?

Is it worth it?

Time heals all wounds.

In your case, it takes about three weeks before you recover fully.

Now you're standing in front of that same booth, same alien in the pink gas, holding out your ticket. You have gotten your photo ID and background check (faked). It warbles behind the security glass.

"Name?"

"Pepper."

"Secondary name?"

You pause.

"Smith."

"The size of your luggage is unusual," it protests.

"It is necessary," you insist. The remains of the important bits of the gyro stand. And some extra devices to shield it from any ShinnCo attempts to make it call home and make your life miserable.

It looks at you.

"Human." The word is unstressed through the speaker. But you know the meaning behind it.

You stare the creature down and wait.

The go-around takes several minutes, but the creature finally tacks on a massive surcharge and lets you through.

Settling into the capsule's launch chair, the long lines of the launch tube visible through the tiny portholes ahead of you, you pull your new overcoat closely around you.

You wonder if Susan can find room for you on her mining ship.

It's a wild non-world out there. One where humans are minorities, alien conglomerates ply the worlds and negotiate with primitives like your own people for their gas giants and extra unused planets. They trade them for space access, advanced technology. Beads and glass many suspect, but not to primitive planets like Earth.

This is your new environment.

ShinnCo you can leave behind.

You reach your hand up and caress the data amulet hanging from your neck. It is the memory of a sandy beach, your back relaxed against a palm tree. The gentle swish of the wind through leaves and water breaking against rocks at the end of the bay soothes you. That's it. A single memory of a life you once wanted to remember back. ShinnCo put a lot of security around it. Your past is the past.

The chair wraps around your waist and comes down your shoulders. You are the person you make yourself to be.

Fifteen seconds.

You are the person you are now.

The whine of the accelerators reaches a crescendo.

You're not going to look into the past and what you were.

Three seconds.

It really isn't important.

Launch.

RESISTANCE

Four days after the coup Stanuel was ordered to fake an airlock pass. The next day he waited inside a cramped equipment locker large enough to hold two people while an armed rover the size and shape of a helmet wafted around the room, twisting and counter-rotating pieces of itself as it scanned the room briefly. Stanuel held his breath and willed himself not to move or make a sound. He just floated in place, thankful for the lack of gravity that might have betrayed him had he needed to depend on locked, nervous muscles.

The rover gave up and returned to the corridor, the airlock door closing behind it. Stanuel slipped back out. The rover had missed him because he'd been fully suited up for vacuum. No heat signature.

Behind the rover's lenses had been the eyes of Pan. And since the coup, anyone knew better than to get noticed by Pan. Even the airlock pass cut it too close. He would disappear when Pan's distributed networks noticed what he'd done.

By then, Pan would not be a problem.

Stanuel checked his suit over again, then cycled the airlock out. The outer door split in two and pulled apart.

But where was the man Stanuel was supposed to bring in?

He realized there was a inky blackness in the space just

outside the ring of the lock. A blotch that grew larger, and then tumbled in. The suit flickered, and turned a dull grey to match the general interior color of the airlock.

The person stood up, and Stanuel repressurized the airlock.

They waited as Stanuel snapped seals and took his own helmet off. He hung the suit up in the locker he'd just hidden in. "We have to hurry, we only have about ten minutes before the next rover patrol."

Behind him, Stanuel heard crinkling and crunching. When he turned around the spacesuit had disappeared. He now faced a tall man with dark skin and long dreadlocks past his shoulders, and eyes as grey as the bench behind him. The spacesuit had turned into a long, black trench-coat. "Rovers?" The man asked.

Stanuel held his hand up and glyphed a three-d picture in the air above his palm. The man looked at the rover spin and twist and shoot. "Originally they were station maintenance bots. Semi-autonomous remote operated vehicles. Now they're armed."

"I see." The man pulled a large backpack off his shoulders and unzipped it.

"So...what now?" Stanuel asked.

The grey eyes flicked up from the pack. "You don't know?"

"I'm part of a cell. But we run distributed tasks, only checking it with people who assign them. It keeps us insulated. I was only told to open this airlock and let you in. You would know what next. Is the attack tonight? Should I get armed? Are you helping the attack?"

The man opened the pack all the way to reveal a small arsenal of guns, grenades, explosives, and oddly: knives. Very large knives. He looked up at Stanuel. "I am the attack. I've been asked to shut Pan down."

"But you're not a programmer..."

"I can do all things through explosives, who destroy for me." The man began moving the contents of the pack inside the pockets and straps of the trenchcoat, clipped more to his belt and thigh, as well as to holsters under each arm, and then added pieces to his ankles.

He was now a walking arsenal.

But only half the pack had been emptied. The mysterious mercenary tossed that at Stanuel. "Besides, you're going to help."

Stanuel coughed. "Me?"

"According to the resistance message, you are a maintenance manager, recently promoted. You still know all the sewer lines, access ducts, and holes required to get me to the tower. How long do you guess we have before it notices your unauthorized use of an airlock?"

"An hour," Stanuel said. The last time he'd accidentally gone somewhere Pan didn't like, rovers had been in his office within an hour.

"And can we get to the tower within an hour, Stanuel, without being noticed?"

Stanuel nodded.

The large, well-armed man pointed at the airlock door into the corridor. "Well, let's not dally."

"Can I ask you something?" Stanuel asked.

"Yes."

"Your name? You know mine. I don't know yours."

"Pepper," said the mercenary. "Now do we get to leave?"

A single tiny sound ended the secrecy of their venture: the buzz of wings. Pepper's head snapped in the direction of the sound, locks spinning out from his head.

He slapped his palm against the side of the wall, crushing a butterfly-like machine perfectly flat.

"A bug," Stanuel said.

Pepper launched down the corridor, bouncing off the walls until he hit the bulkhead at the far end. He glanced around the corner. "Clear."

"Pan knows you're in Haven know." Stanuel felt fear bloom,

an instant explosion of paralysis that left him hanging in the air. "It will mobilize."

"Then get me into the tower, quick. Let's go, Stanuel, we're not engaged in something that rewards the slow."

But Stanuel remained in place. "They chose me because I had no family," he said. "I had less to lose. I would help them against Pan. But..."

Pepper folded his arms. "It's already seen you. You're already dead."

That sunk in. Stanuel had handled emergencies. Breaches, where vacuum flooded in, sucking the air out. He'd survived explosions, dumb mistakes, and even being speared by a piece of rebar. All by keeping cool and doing what needed done.

He hadn't expected, when told that he'd need to let in an assassin, that'd he get this involved. But what did he expect? That he could be part of the resistance and not ever risk his life? He'd risked it the moment one of his co-workers had started whispering him to him, talking about overthrowing Pan, and he'd only stood there and listened.

Stanuel took a deep breath and nodded. "Okay. I'm sorry."

The space station Haven was a classic wheel, rotating slowly to provide some degree of gravity for its inhabitants so that they did not have to lose bone mass and muscle, the price of living in no gravity.

At Haven's center lay the hub. Here lay an atrium, the extraordinary no-gravity gardens and play areas for Haven's citizens. Auditoriums and pools and labs and tourist areas and fields, the heart of the community. Dripping down from the hub, docking ports, airlocks, antennae, and spare mass from the original asteroid Haven had taken its metals. This was where they floated now.

But on the other side of the hub hung a long and spindly structure that had once housed the central command for the station. A bridge, of sorts, with a view of all of Haven, sat at the very tip of the tower. The bridge was duplicated just below in the form of an observation deck and restaurant for visitors and proud citizens and school trips.

All things the tower existed for in that more innocent time before.

Now Pan sat in the bridge, looking out at all of them, both through the large portal-like windows up there, and through the network of rovers and insect cams scattered throughout Haven.

One of which Pepper had just flattened.

Stanuel knew they no longer had an hour now.

Pepper squatted in front of the hatch. "It's good I'm not claustrophobic."

"This runs all the way to the restaurant at the tower. It's the fastest way there."

"If we don't choke on fumes and grease first." Pepper scraped grease off the inside.

Stanuel handed him a mask with filters from the tiny utility closet underneath the pipe. He also found a set of headlamps. "Get in, I'll follow, we need to hurry."

Pepper hauled himself into the tube and Stanuel followed, worming his way in. When he closed the hatch after them the darkness seemed infinite until Pepper clicked a tiny penlight on.

Moving down the tube was simple enough. They were in the hub. They were weightless. They could use their fingertips to slowly move their way along.

After several minutes Pepper asked, voice muffled by the filter, "so how did it happen? Haven was one of the most committed to the idea of techno-democracy."

There were hundreds of little bubbles of life scattered all throughout the asteroid belt, hidden away from the mess of Earth and her orbit by distance and anonymity. Each one a petri dish of politics and culture. Each a pearl formed around a bit of asteroid dirt that birthed it.

"There are problems with a techno-democracy," muttered Stanuel. "If you're a purist, like we were, you had to have the citizenry decide on everything." The sheer amount of things that a society needed decided had almost crushed them.

Every minute everyone had to decide something. Pass a new law. Agree to send delegates to another station. Accept taxes. Divvy out taxes. Pay a bill. The stream of decisions became overwhelming, constantly popping up and requiring and electronic yes or no. And research was needed for each decision.

"The artificial intelligence modelers came up with our solution. They created intelligences that would vote just as you would if it had the time to do nothing but focus on voting." They weren't real artificial intelligences. The modelers took your voting record, and paired it to your buying habits, social habits, and all the other aspects of your life that were tracked in modern life to model your habits. After all, if a bank could use a financial profile to figure out if an unusual purchase didn't reflect the buyer's habits and freeze an account for safety reasons, why couldn't the same black box logic be applied to a voter's patterns?

Pepper snorted. "You turned over your voting to machines."

Stanuel shook his head, making the headlamp's light dart from side to side. "Not machines. Us. The profiles were incredible. They also modeled what votes were important enough or that the profilers were uncertain to get right that they only passed on the important ones to us. They were like spam filters. They freed us from the incredible flood of meaningless minutiae that the daily running of a government needed."

"But they failed," Pepper grunted.

"Yes and no..."

"Quiet." Pepper pointed his penlight down. "I hear something. Clinking around back the way we came from."

"Someone chasing us?"

"No. It's mechanical."

Stanuel thought about it for a moment. He couldn't think of anything. "Rover?"

Pepper stopped and Stanuel collided with his boots. "So our time has run out."

"I don't know."

A faint clang echoed around them. "Back up," Pepper said, pushing him away with a quick shove of the boot to the top of his head.

"What are you doing?"

"We've come far enough." Four extremely loud bangs filled the tube with absurdly bright flashes of light. Pepper moved out through the ragged rip in the pipe.

Another large wall blocked him. "What is this?"

Stanuel, still blinking, looked at it from still inside the pipe. "You'll want the other side. Nothing but vacuum on the other side." Had Pepper used more explosive they might have just been blown right out the side of Haven.

"Right." Pepper twisted further out, and another explosion rocked the pipe.

When Stanuel wriggled out and around the tube he saw trees. They'd blown a hole in the lawn of the gardens. They carefully climbed out, pushing past dirt, and the tubes and support equipment that monitored and maintained the gardens and soaked the roots with water.

"Now what?" Stanuel asked. "We're going to be seen."

"Now it gets messy," Pepper said. He pulled Stanuel along toward the large elevator at the center. "I'm going with a frontal assault. It'll be messy. But...I do well at messy."

"There's no reason for me to be here, then," Stanuel said. "What use will I be? I failed to get you there through the exhaust pipes. Why not just let me go?"

Pepper laughed. "Not quite ready to die for the cause, Stanuel?"

"No. Yes. I'm not sure, it just feels like suicide, and I'm not sure who that helps."

"You're safer with me." Pepper launched them from branch to branch through the trees. Now that curfews were in effect, no families perched in the great globe of green, kids screaming and racing through the trees. It was eerily silent.

Pepper slowed them down in the last grove of trees before the elevators at the core of the gardens. As they gently floated towards the lobby at the bottom of the shaft three well-built men, the kind who obviously trained their bodies up on the rim of the wheel, turned the corner.

They carried stun guns. Non-lethal, but still menacing.

Stanuel heard a click. Pepper held out a gun in each hand. Real guns, perfectly lethal.

"I'd turn those off," Pepper said, "and pass them over, and then no-one would get hurt."

They hesitated. But then the commanding voice of Pan filled the gardens. "Do as he says. And then escort him to me."

They looked at each other, unhappy, and tossed the guns over. Pepper threw them off into the trees. "You're escorting us?"

The three unhappy security men nodded. "Pan says you have an electro-magnetic pulse weapon. We're not to provoke you."

Stanuel bit his lip. It felt like a trap. These traitors were taking them into the maw of the beast, and Pepper, as far as he could see, looked cheerful about it. "It's a trap," he muttered.

"Well of course it is," Pepper said. "But it's a good one that avoids us skulking about, getting dirtier, or having to shoot our way through." The mercenary followed Pan's lackeys into the elevator. He turned and looked at Stanuel, hovering outside. "And Pan's right. I do have an E.M.P device. But if I trigger it this deep into the hub, I take out all your power generating capabilities and computer core systems."

"Really?" Stanuel was intrigued.

Pepper held up a tiny metal tube with a button on the end. "If I get to the tower," Pepper said. "I can trigger it and take out Pan, while leaving the rest of the station unaffected."

Stanuel had weathered five days of his beloved Haven under the autocratic rule of Pan, the trickster.

He'd travel with Pepper to see it end, he realized.

He pulled himself into the elevator.

For five days Haven's populace had a ruler, a single being who's word was law, who's thoughts were made policy. Pan stood in the center of the command console, it's face lit by the light of a hundred screens and the reflections off the inner rim of Haven's great wheel.

Pan wore a simple blue suit, had tan skin, brown eyes, and brown hair. His androgynous face and thin body meant that had he stood in a crowd of Haven's citizens, he would hardly have been noticed. He could be anybody, or everybody.

He also flickered slightly as he turned.

"My executioner and his companion. I'm delighted," Pan said. "If I could shake your hand, I would." He gave a slight bow.

Pepper returned it.

Pan smiled. "I've been waiting for you two for quite a while. I apologize for sending the rover up the exhaust pipe."

Pepper shrugged. "No matter. So what now? I have something that can take you out, you have me surrounded by nasty surprises..."

Pan folded its arms. "I don't do nasty surprises, Pepper. I'm not a monster, contrary to what Stanuel might say. You have an E.M.P device, and if you were to set it off further down the tower, you would shut all Haven down. True, I have backup capabilities that mitigate that, but your device presents a terrible risk to the well being of the citizenry. With the device and you up here, the only risk is to me."

An easy enough decision, Stanuel thought. Trigger the damn device! But Pepper glanced around the room, maybe seeing traps that Stanuel couldn't. "If you don't do nasty surprises, what stops me from zapping you out, right here, right now?"

"I would like to make you an offer. If you'd listen."

Pepper's lips quirked. "I wouldn't be much of a mercenary if I just accepted the higher bid in the middle of the job. You don't get repeat work very often that way."

Pan held its hands up. "I understand. But consider this, I am, indirectly, the one who hired you."

Stanuel had to object. "The resistance..."

"I run it," Pan smiled. "I know everything it does, who it hires, and in many cases, I give it the orders."

Stanuel felt like he'd been thrown into a freezing cold vat of water. He lost his breath. "What do you mean? You infiltrated it?" They had lost, even before they'd started.

Pan turned to the mercenary. "Stanuel is bewildered, as are many, by what they created, Pepper. I'm merely the amalgamated avatar of the converged will of all the simulations made to run this colony. The voter simulations kept taking up energy, so the master processing program came up with a more elegant solution: me. Why run millions of emulators, when it could fuse them all into a single expression of its will that would run the government?"

"A clever solution," Pepper said.

"A techno-democracy, even more so than the vanilla kind, is messy. With study committees and votes on everything, things that needed done quickly didn't get done in time. Dangerously so.

"So the emulations decided to put forward a bill for vote, buried in the middle of some other obscure administrivia. The vote was that emulations be given command of the government."

Stanuel stepped forward. "We woke up and found that in a single moment all of Haven had been disenfranchised."

"By your own desires and voting predictive records," Pan said. "In a way, yes. In a way, no."

Stanuel spit at the dictatorial hologram in front him. "Then the emulators decided that a single amalgamation, an avatar, and expression of all their wills, would work better. So then even our own voting patterns turned over their power."

"Not surprising," Pepper said. "You didn't have the maturity to keep your own vote, you turned it over to the copies of yourselves. Why be surprised that the copies would do something similar and turn to a benevolent dictator of their own creation?"

Pan looked pleased. "Dictators aren't so bad, if they're the right dictator. And it's hard coded into my very being to look out for the community. That's why I look like this," it waved a hand over its face. "I'm the average of all the faces in Haven. Political poll modeling shows that were I to run for office, if would be almost guaranteed based on physiological responses alone."

Stanuel looked at Pepper. "Pan may have infiltrated, but you were still paid to destroy it. Do it."

"No," Pan said. "You might pull that trigger. But if you do, you destroy what all Haven really wanted, what it desired, and what it worked very hard to create, Pepper, even if they didn't realize they consciously wanted it."

"I've heard you get the government you deserve," Pepper said. "But this is something else. They all created their own tyranny..."

"But Pepper, I'm not a tyrant. If they vote as a whole to oust me, they can do it."

Pepper moved over to the one of great windows to look out at the inside rim of Haven. Thousands of distant portholes dotted the giant wheel, lit up by the people living inside the rooms across from them.

"Look around you," Pan implored. "There are plenty who like what I'm doing. I'm rebuilding parts of Haven that have sat in neglect for years. I'm improving agriculture as we speak. I've made the choices that were hard, got things into motion that just sat there while people quibbled over them. I am action. I am progress."

Stanuel kicked forward and Pepper glanced back at him. "I think Stanuel objects."

Pan sighed. "Yes, a few will be disaffected. They will always be disaffected. That was why I created outlets for the disaffected, because they are a part of me as well. But my plea to you, Pepper, is not to break this great experiment. I can offer you more money, a place of safety here whenever you would want it, and Haven as a powerful ally to your needs."

Pepper nodded and sat in the air, his legs folded. "I have a question."

"Proceed."

"Why do they call you Pan?"

"They call me Pan because it's short for panopticon. An old experiment: if you were to create a round jail with a tower in the center, with open cell walls facing it, and the ability to look into every cell, you would have the ultimate surveillance society. The panopticon. In some ways, Haven is just that, with me at its center."

Pepper chuckled. "I'd half expected some insane military dictator wearing a head of antlers calling himself Pan."

Pan did not laugh. It leaned closer. "Pepper, understand me. This is not your fight. I'm the naturally elected ruler of Haven. The choice to remove me, that isn't yours. I did not bring you here to destroy me, but for other reasons."

"The choice?" The word affected Pepper in some way Stanuel could not figure out. He looked over at Stanuel. "Then if you're a benevolent ruler, you will escort me off Haven, leave Stanuel alive, and move on to other things. After all, it was your orders that set Stanuel down this path."

"Of course. It's that or a sentence in one of Haven's residential rooms. You'll be locked in, but comfortable. There do have to be ways to handle such things. Exile, or confinement."

"Okay, Mr. Pan. Okay. My work here is done." Pepper moved towards Stanuel with a flick of his feet. "Come on Stanuel, it's time to leave the tower."

Stanuel could hardly look Pepper in the eye. "I can't believe you left there."

"Pan made a good argument."

"Pan offered to pay you more. That's all."

"There's that, but I won't take it." Pepper scratched his head. "If I destroyed Pan, what would you do?"

Stanuel frowned. "What do you mean?"

"You said the emulations wouldn't be allowed to hold direct control, earlier. Does that mean you'd allow the emulations to come back and decide votes for you?"

"One assumes. We might have not gotten them right, but if we can fix that error, things can go back to the way they were."

Pepper unpacked his suit and stepped into it. It crinkled and cracked as he zipped it up. "And then I'll be back. Because you'll repeat the same patter all over again."

"What?"

"For all your assumptions, you're not quite seeing the pattern. Deep down, somewhere, you all want Pan. You don't want the responsibility of voting, you want the easy result."

"That's not true," Stanuel objected.

"Oh come on. Think of all the times princes and princesses are adored and feted. Thing of all the actors and great people we adore and fawn over."

"That doesn't make us slavish followers."

Pepper cocked his head. "No, but we still can't escape the instincts we carry from being a small band of hunter-gatherers making their way across a plain, depending on a single leader who knew the ins and outs of their tiny tribe and listened to their feedback. That doesn't scale, so we have inelegant hacks around it.

"Stanuel, you all created a technological creature, able to view you all and listen to all your feedback, and embody a benevolent single tribal leader. Not only was it born out of your unconscious needs, even your own emulations overwhelmingly voted it into power as sole ruler of Haven."

Stanuel raised his hand. "That's all true, and over the last four days we've argued around all this when we found out about the vote. But, Pepper, whether perfect or not, we can't allow a single person to rule us. It goes against everything we believe in, everything we worked for when we created Haven."

Pepper nodded. "I know."

"And you're going to walk away."

"I have to. Because this wasn't some power grab, it was the will of your people. There was a vote. Pan is right, it is rightful ruler. But," Pepper raised a hand, "I'm not leaving you empty-handed."

"What do you mean?"

He handed over the backpack and pressed a small stick with a button into Stanuel's hand. "The E.M.P device is in the backpack. You won't get anywhere near the tower to take out just Pan, but if you trigged it in the hub after I leave, it will shut Haven down. Pan will have backups, and his supporters will protect the tower, but if enough people feel like you do, you can storm it with the guns in that pack."

"You're asking me to...fight?"

"You know your history. The tree of liberty needs watered with some blood every now and then, Thomas Jefferson I think said that. Most of your ancestors fought for it. You could have kept it, had you just...taken the time to vote yourself instead of leaving it to something else."

"I don't know if I can." Stanuel was bewildered. He'd never done anything violent in his life.

Pepper smiled. "You might find Pan is more willing to fold than you imagine. Think about it."

With that, he stepped into the airlock. The door shut with a hiss, and the spacesuit faded into camouflage black as Pepper disappeared to get back into whatever stealth ship had bought him to Haven.

Stanuel stood there. He pulled the backpack's straps up over onto his shoulders and made his way towards the gardens, mulling over the mercenary's last words.

A hologram of Pan waited for him at the entrance to the gardens, but with no goons nearby. Stanuel had expected to be captured, with the threat of a long confinement ahead of him. But it was just the electronic god of Haven and Stanuel.

"You didn't understand what he meant, did you?" Pan said. It really was the panopticon, listening to everything that happened in Haven.

"No." Stanuel held the switch to the E.M.P in his hand, waiting for some trick. Was he going to get shot in the head by a sniper? But Pan said it didn't use violence.

Maybe a tranquilizer dart of some sort?

"I told you," Pan said, "I also created the resistance."

"But that doesn't make any sense," Stanuel said.

"It does if you stop thinking of me as a person, but as an avatar of your collective emulators. Every ruling system has an opposition, the day after I was voted into power, I had to create a series of checks and balances against myself. That was the resistance."

"But I was recruited by people."

"And they were recruited by my people, working for me, who were told it was to create a tame opposition as a honey trap." Pan flickered as he walked through a tree. An incongruous vision, as Stanuel floated through the no gravity garden.

"Why would you want to die?"

"Because, I may not be what all of you want, just what most of you want. I have to create an opportunity for me to be stopped, or else, I really am a tyrant and not the best solution. That is why Pepper was hired to bring the E.M.P device aboard. That was why, ultimately, he left it with you."

"So it's all in my hands," Stanuel said.

"Yes. Live in a better economy, a safer economy, but one ruled by what you have created. Or muddle along yourselves." Pan moved in front of Stanuel, floating with him.

Stanuel held up the metal tube and hovered his thumb over the button. "Men should be free."

Pan nodded sadly. "But Stanuel, you all will never be able to get things done the way I can. It will be such a mess of compromise, personality, mistakes, wrong choices, emotional choices, mob rule, and imperfect decisions. You could well destroy

Haven with your imprecise decisions."

It was a siren call. But even though Pan was perfect, and right, it was the same song that led smart men to call tyrants leaders and do so happily. The promise of quick action, clean and fast decisions.

Alluring.

"I know it will be messy," Stanuel said, voice quavering. "And I have no idea how it will work out. But at least it will be ours."

He made his choice and pressed the button. He watched as the lights throughout Haven dimmed and flickered. Pan disappeared with a sigh, a ghost banished. The darkness marched its glorious way through the cavernous gardens toward Stanuel, who folded up in the air by a tree while he waited for the dark to take him in its freeing embrace.

A COLD HEART

In the mining facility's automated sickbay she'd put her metal hand on your chest and said, "I'm sorry." The starry glinting fragments of ice and debris bounced around the portholes. Twinkling like stars, but shaken loose of their spots in the dark vacuum.

They shot her hand, but she had pushed the raiders right back off her claim. The asteroid was still bagged and tagged as her own to prospect. You never told her they were all dead now, mere bloodstains on the corridors of Ceres, but one imagines she suspects as much.

"I have a cold hand, but you have a cold heart," she had said. "I can't love a cold heart."

And it's true.

Strange place to part ways, but she's been thinking about it for a while. Susan knows her path.

"You'll keep hunting for your memories?" she asks. "That corporate data fence?"

You nod. "I'll have more time on my hands."

It's a strange thing to image a whole brain down to the quantum level. Crack a person apart and bolt stronger skeletal system into him. Refashion him into a machine, a weapon to be used for one's gain. Then burn the memories out. Use the lie of getting them back as a lure to make that human serve you. But stranger things had been done during the initial occupation of Earth.

Now you'll be having those back. You want to know who you were.

You want more than just the one they left you to whet your appetite.

Your first encounter with the *Xaymaca Pride*'s crew is an intense-looking engineer. Small scabs on her shaved head show she's sloppy with a blade, and there's irritation around the eye sockets, where a sad looking metal eye has been welded into the skin somewhere in a cheap bodyshop.

"You're the mercenary," she says. "Pepper."

You're both hanging in the air inside the lock. The pressure differential slightly pushes at your ears. You crack your jaw, left, right, and the pressure ceases. The movement causes your dreadlocks to shift around you, tapping the side of your face.

"I'm not on a job," you tell her. "I don't work for anyone anymore."

But you used to. And there's a reputation. It's spread in front of you like a bow wave. Dopplering around, varying in intensity here and there.

Five years working with miners, stripping ore from asteroids enveloped in plastic bags and putting in sweat-work, and all anyone knows about is the old wetwork. Stuff that should have been left to the shadows. Secrets never meant for civilians.

But that shit didn't fly out in the tight tin-cans floating around the outer solar system. Everyone had their noses in everyone else's business.

"The captain wants to see you before detach."

Probably having second thoughts, you think. Been hard to find a way to get out of the system, because the new rulers of the worlds here want you dead for past actions. You can skulk around the fringes, or even go back to Earth and hide in the packed masses and cities.

But to go interstellar: you eventually get noticed when you're one of the trickle of humanity leaving to the other forty eight habitable worlds. Particularly if you're one of the few that's not a servant of the various alien species that are now the overlords of humanity.

The bridge crew all twist in place to get a good look at you when you float into the orb-shaped cockpit at the deep heart of the cylindrical starship. They're all lined up on one plane of the cockpit, the orb able to gimbal with the ship's orientation to orient them to the pressures of high acceleration.

Not common on an average container ship. Usually those were little more than a set of girders cargo could get slotted into with a living area on one end and engines on the other.

The captain hangs in the air, eyes drowned in shipboard internal information, but now he stirs and looks at you. His skin is brown, like yours. Like many of the crew's. From what you've heard, they all hail from the Caribbean. DeBrun has been smuggling people out of the solar system to points beyond for a whole year now.

"I'm John deBrun," he says. "You're Pepper."

You regard him neutrally.

DeBrun starts the conversation jovially. "In order to leave the solar system, I need anti-matter, Pepper. And no one makes it but the Satraps. Who sell it only to those they like. They own interstellar commerce, and most of the planets in the solar system. And according to the bastard aliens, you do not have interstellar travel privileges. I've let you aboard, to ask you a question, face to face."

You raise an eyebrow. It's a staged meeting. DeBrun is putting on a show for the bridge crew. "Yes?"

"Why should I smuggle you from here to Nova Terra's Orbital?"

A moment passes as you seem to consider that, letting deBrun's little moment stretch out. "It'll piss off the satraps, and I'll wait long enough so that it's not obvious you're the ship that slipped me in."

DeBrun dramatically considers that, rubbing his chin. "How will you do that?"

"I'm going to steal something from a satrap."

"Steal what?"

"My memories," you tell him.

DeBrun grins. "Okay. We'll take you."

"Just like that?"

"You know who we are, what we're planning to do?"

You nod. "An exodus. To find a new world, free of the Satrapy."

"Not to find," deBrun says. "We found it. We just need to get there again, with five ships. And having you distract the satrap at our rally point... well, I like that. There are a lot of people hiding on that habitat, waiting to get loaded up while we fuel. The first people of a whole new world, a new society. You should join."

"The satrap at your rally point has something I want."

"So I've heard. Okay. Jay, shut the locks, clear us out. Our last passenger is on board."

Jay and DeBrun could be brothers. Same smile. Though you're not sure. You don't look at people that much anymore. Not since Susan. You don't care anymore. You can explore the fleshy side of what remains of you after you get the memories back.

Because they will make you whole again.

The ship's cat adopts you. It hangs in the air just above the nape of your neck, and whenever the ship adjusts its flight patch claws dig into the nape of your neck.

Claws, it seems, are a benefit in zero gravity.

Now matter how many times you toss the furball off down the corridor it finds its way back into your room.

How many wormholes between Earth and Nova Terra? You lose track of the stomach-lurching transits as the cylindrical ship burns its way upstream through the network.

You dream about the one memory you still have. The palm tree, sand in your toes.

It could have been a vacation, that beach. But the aquamarine colors just inside the reef feel like home. It's why, when you heard the shipboard accents you followed crew back to this ship and chose it. The oil-cooked johnny cakes, pate, curry, rice... muscle memory and habit leave you thinking you came from the islands.

You don't know them. But they are your people.

At Nova Terra, slipping out via an airlock and a liberated spacesuit, you look back at the pockmarked outer shell of the ship. It's nestled against the massive, goblet-shaped alien habitat orbiting Nova Terra's purplish atmosphere, itself circling the gas giant Medea. The few hundred free humans who live here call the glass and steel cup-shaped orbital Hope's End.

You're a long way from home now. Hundreds of wormholes away, each of them many lightyears of jumps. Each wormhole a transit point in a vast network that patch together the various worlds the Satrapy rules over.

Too far to stop now. You only were able to come one way. This wasn't a round trip ticket. You'll have to figure out how to get back home later.

Once you have memories. Once you know exactly where that palm tree was, you'll have something to actually go back for.

The woman who sits at the table across from you a week later does so stiffly, and yet with such a sense of implied ownership that your back tenses. There's something puppet-like, and you know the strings are digital. Hardware buried into this one's neuro-cortex allow something else to ride shotgun.

Something.

She's in full thrall, eyes glinting with an alien intelligence behind them. The satrap of Hope's End has noticed your arrival and walked one of his human ROVs out to have a chat. That it took it two days for it to notice you, when you've just been sitting out in the open all this time, demonstrates a level of amateurishness for its kind.

Then again, Hope's End is sort of the satrapy's equivalent of a dead end position. A small assignment on a small habitat in orbit. The real players live down the gravity well, on the juicy planets.

"I know who you are," the woman says. Around you free humans in gray paper suits stream to work in the distant crevices of the station. Life is hard on Hope's End, you can tell just by their posture. The guarded faces, the invisible heaviness on the shoulders.

You say nothing to the woman across from you.

"You are here without permission. Do you know you I could have you killed for that?"

"You could try that," you say. "The cost would be high."

"Oh, I imagine." She leans back, and flails an arm in what must be some far-off alien physical expression badly translated. There is a pit, a cavern, somewhere deep in the bowels of Hope's End. Somewhere with three quarter's gravity, and a dirt pit, and a massive recreation pool. And slopping around is a giant wormy trilobite of an alien. "I know a lot about you. More than you know about yourself."

Indeed.

The thing you need is that cavern's location.

Until you get that, everything is a dance. A game. A series of feints and jabs. Your life is the price of a single misstep.

But what do you have to lose? You don't know. Because you can't remember. It was taken from you. The satrap owns everything you would lose by dying. You're already dead, you think.

"So why haven't you killed me?" you ask the satrap.

"The *Xaymaca Pride*," it says. "They're sneaking people around my habitat. As if I wouldn't notice. And they're hoping to leave… for a new world."

"You believe deBrun's propaganda?" you ask. Because even you don't half believe it. The man is slightly messianic. He's probably going to lead them all to their deaths, so far from Earth. Alone among uncaring, hard aliens the likes of which haven't even bothered to make it to Earth.

The Satrapy is vast. Hundreds of wormhole junctions between each habitable world, and dozens and dozens of those linked up. And the Satraps hold the navigation routes to themselves. The few individual ships out there blunder around and retrace their steps and are lucky they're not shot down by the Satrapy's gun banks in the process.

"DeBrun destroyed his own ship upon return from the Fringes," the woman says. "He has memorized the location in his head."

"Ah. So you believe it is true." A ship. There were corporations on Earth that couldn't afford an interstellar ship. Not a small act, destroying one.

"Many people raised funds to create this… Black Starliner Corporation's fleet," the satrap's thrall says. "I believe the world he found is real. Unspoiled and real. And I want it for myself." That last bit is lashed out. There is hunger in that statement, and a hint of frustration.

This satrap is trapped up here, while its siblings cavort on the surface of Nova Terra. They have thousands of humans and aliens in thrall at their disposal, chipped with neurotech that let them create an army of servants they can remote control around with mere thought.

"I am stuck in this boring, metal cage. But I have great plans. Would you like to know how you got that scar above your left inner thigh? The jagged one, that is faded because you've had it since you were a teenager?"

You stop breathing for a second. Unconsciously you run a hand down and trace the zig-zag pattern with your thumb.

"You were climbing a fence. Barbed wire curled around the top, and you were trying to get over it into a field. You slipped. You were so scared, for a split second, as it ripped open your leg. The blood was so bright in the sun, and the ground tumbled up toward you as fell, in shock."

When you break the stare, you've lost a little battle of the wills. "So you do have them."

"I love collecting the strangest things," the satrap said through the woman. Now that you are paying attention, you see that her hair is unwashed, and that there are sores above her clavicle. "I have two thousand humans, in thrall to me. Many other species as well. And I've used these eyes to pry, sneak, and attempt my way on board. I want John deBrun. I'm tired of watching these free humans skulk about."

"So go pick him up," you say.

"Oh, yes. I want to sink my tendrils into deBrun's fleshy little mind and suck those coordinates out. But he remains on that damn ship, with guards ever at the airlocks. I've learned he has protocols for an attack, and anything I can do leaves me too high a risk of him dying in a large attack. So I want you to bring me John deBrun. It is the sort of thing, I'm told, you are good at."

"And in exchange you give me my memories back?"

"You're every bit as sharp as your memories indicate you ever were," the woman says, and stands up.

"What if I refuse? What if I go after the memories myself?" you smile.

"You are alone, on a station, where only a few hold their own freedom. Every other eye in here is in thrall to me. Most of the time, they are free to engage in their petty lives, but the moment I desire, I could command them all to rip you from limb to limb with their bare hands. I considered it. But I think instead, we will both be happier if you bring John deBrun to level A7. Portal fourteen.

My security forces will be waiting."

And there is your way in.

You wait in the shadows.

You've often been something that goes bump in the night.

The satraps consider themselves gods to the species they rule over. But sometimes, gods want other gods killed. In theory their reasons are arcane and unknowable. But as far as you can tell they are the usual: jealousy. Covetousness. A desire for more power.

Sometimes gods want other gods to die, and you decided you didn't just want to go bump in the night and scare people. You decided you could aim higher than being just a human assassin. And when the satrap of Mars decided it wanted the blue jewel of Earth, you let it sharpen you into a weapon the likes of which few wished to imagine.

All that gooey alien nanotechnology that burrowed through your pores, all that power...

Behold the giant slayer, you once thought, looking in the mirror.

You weren't supposed to live, but even jealous alien eyes from the dusty red ruin of Mars couldn't imagine the hells you would face to continue feeding your quest. It had no idea the depths of your anger. The strength of your resolve.

It didn't know you had such a cold, cold heart, and that it had helped make it so much colder. You were already steel, and artificial sinew. It only furthered a transformation that had begun long ago.

The gun that John deBrun points at your head when he comes into his quarters is capable of doing much more than give you a headache. He's good. Knew you were in the room. Maybe considered flushing out this part of the ship, but instead comes in to talk.

He's keeping his distance though.

"You're here for the coordinates, aren't you?" he asks.

You nod. "I am."

You keep your hands in the air and sit down. You want John as comfortable as possible.

"If it's not me, someone else will come. They'll cut your head off and run it back to the satrap. What I have in mind is a little different."

John shakes his head sadly. He lifts up his shirt to show several puckered scars. "You're not the first to try. We have systems in place to deal with this. Every possible variable. I have to assume that everyone is trying to stop me. Other humans, my own crew, people at Hope's End. I'm tougher than they realize."

"You'll want to do this my way," you say.

"And why is that?"

"Because it is happening, John. This right now is happening: I will take you to the satrap. Because I have come too far, and done too many things, to not go there and get my memories back. Nothing else matters to me. Not you, your ships, your cause, the people in this habitat. There is nothing for me there. There is everything in the satrap's den."

John shakes his head. "Do you know how much they've taken from us? You think your memories are the worst of it? Let me lay down some history on you: there's always been someone taking it away. They took it away from people like us when we were transported across an ocean. Taken away when aliens landed and ripped our countries away from us. Claimed our planets. There's a long, long list of things ripped away from people in history. You are not alone."

"Unlike them," you say, "what was taken from me is just within reach now."

"At a price," John says.

"Everything has a price," you say, moving toward him.

John blinks, surprised. He's been thinking we were having a dialogue, but you were waiting for the gun to dip slightly. For his attention to waver.

He's a good shot. Hits you right in the chest. A killing shot. One that would have stopped anyone else. The round penetrates, explodes. Shrapnel shreds the place a heart usually rests.

But that is just one small part. One bloodstream.

That faint hiccup of backup pumps dizzies you slightly as your blood pressure shifts and adapts. You cough blood, and grab John. You break his hand as you disarm him and knock him out.

For a while you sit next to him, the horrible feeling in your chest filling you with waves of pain.

Eventually that ebbs. You evaluate the damage, glyphs and messages ghosting across your eyeballs as your body, more alien machine than human, begins to process the damage and heal itself.

You won't be facing the satrap in optimal fighting condition.

But you're so close. And if you delay, you invite the risk of the satrap sending someone for John. That could be messy. And it won't give you the one thing you really want out of all this: an invitation into the satrap's personal cavern, deep past its layers of defenses.

Hello there you slimey alien shit, you're thinking. I've got a treat for you.

Just come a little closer, and don't mind the big teeth behind this smile.

You snap the ammonia capsule apart under John's nose and he jerks awake. You're both in a loading bay near the rim of Hope's End. Water drips off in a corner, and the industrial grit on the walls is old and faded. A section of the habitat that has fallen into disuse.

"Don't do this. You should join us, Pepper. Leave all this behind. Start something fresh."

"That's not what's happening right now," you say. "The direction of this journey was set a long time ago." The door at the far end of the bay creaks open.

"You can't kill a satrap," he says.

You lean next to him. "Your ships, they were never going to leave Hope's End. The satrap here gave you enough fuel to bring those people here. But right now, you're being given dribs and drabs of antimatter. Enough to go back and from to Earth. But not enough to make it back where you want to go with a whole fleet, right?"

John is silent.

You laugh. "The creature strings you along, until it can get what it wants. And then every single person who came here, well, they'll truly understand the name the few hundred free humans scraping by here gave it. Won't they? Hope's End. Because even if you're free, you're not free of the satrap's long arm. And you'll be the one who lured them here with tales of a free world."

John lets out a deep breath, and slumps forward.

"But listen to me. Work with me, and I'll help you get what you need. Do you understand?"

"Neither of us will walk away alive from this," John says. "We are both dead men. We're talking, but we are dead men."

The empty-eyed vassals of the satrap encircle you, a watchful, coordinated crowd that sighs happily as their eyes confirm that you have indeed delivered John deBrun.

"I want my memories, now," you say, holding tight to John. "Come with us."

Somewhere deep inside, hope stirs. Anticipation builds.

Caution, you warn.

You're both herded deep into Hope's End by ten humans in thrall to the satrap. Away from the green commons, below the corridors, below the subways and utility pipes, out of storage, and into the core ballast in the heart of the structure. The shadows are everywhere, and fluids drip slowly in the reduced gravity.

Muck oozes from grates, and biological mists hang in the air, thick on the lungs.

The satrap's subterranean cavern is dim, and the wormy trilobite itself slouched in a dust pit at the center. The long tendrils around its maw socketed into machines, and from those machines, controlled anyone unfortunate enough to be in thrall.

A curious adaption. You imagine the satrap evolved somewhere deep underground, where it could lie in weight and plunge it's neuro-tendrils into a prey's spine. And then what? It could use predators to grab prey, without harm to itself? Use prey as lures, dangling around that eager, gaping mouth.

"Finally," all ten voices around you say in unison.

John is shoved to the floor in front of you, and you move into the next section of your plan. You reach up to your back and use carbon-fibre fingernails to rip into the scars on your back.

This hurts.

But pain doesn't last forever. Not the pain of your skin ripping apart, or your fingers pulling. The pain of grabbing the handle just underneath as you pull the modified machete of your shoulder blade with a wet, tearing and hiss.

Memory strata reforms the blade's handle to fit your grasp, and the black edge of the blade sucks the light into it. The molecular surface is hydrophobic, the viscera and blood on it slide off and splash to the floor.

The satrap's thralls move toward you, but you put the edge of the short blade against the back of John's skull. "Don't."

As one, they all pull back.

You could have killed John with your bare hands, you don't need the sword. This is part statement. Theatre to help the satrap realize that you're far more dangerous than it has realized. Because, if it can get away with it, the satrap will have both its prize and keep your memories.

And that isn't going to be happening.

"Give me my memories," you tell it.

"Let me have my new world," it replies in ten voices.

Ten. That's all it has surrounding you.

But you want those memories, so the stand off continues. You broadcast your implacability. You will not be moving until you are given those memories. And first.

"Tell it half the coordinates," you order John. You push the edge of the machete against his neck. Let's dangle the prize a little, you think.

"No," John says firmly.

"John," you kneel next to him. And you whisper, "it will die with those coordinates in its head. Trust me. Don't hold it to just yourself now, let it go. Let go of the burden. Let me help you. And then this will be all over."

But you notice something in his response.

He has been sharing the burden. Someone else knows the coordinates. Who? His first mate. Jay. There was a bond there, you remember.

John stumbles to his feet. "If you want the coordinates, you'll have to rip them out of my head yourself," he says to the satrap.

And why would he do that?

His body is warm, near feverish. A satrap wouldn't notice. Not a satrap that had people under thrall to it with sores on their skin. But you notice.

You're not the only player in this game. John has a different plan. A plan to protect the coordinates. A plan to give his people time to grab what they need: fuel. He's got a bomb in him. Hidden, like your machete.

Well done, Mr. deBrun, you think.

Something moves from in the shadows. A large man with shaggy hair, seven and a half feet tall, muscle and fat and pistoned machine all stitched together like an art show gone wrong. A glimpse of what you could have been, if you'd been designed for strength and strength alone.

In the palm of his oversized hand, a brick that leaked superconducting fluid. ShinnCo logo on the outside and all. The last time you saw it... the last time you saw it, you'd woken up in a room and a man in a suit had sat with it in his lap. He'd explained to you that you were in that box. Everything that had once been you, at least. And now they owned it. And by extension, you.

"A copy of your memories," the satrap says. "You'll hand deBrun over. I know you. I have tasted your memories. Partaken of you."

"You know who I was, know who I am," you say. "That was the me before, I'm the me after they took all that, sliced me apart, rebuilt me, and deployed me."

You grab John's head, and before anyone in the cavern can twitch, you slice his head off and hold it up into the air. John's body slumps forward, blood fountaining out over the rock at your feet.

"How long before the dying neurons are inaccessible in here?" you shout.

Everything in the room is flailing, responding to the movements of the satrap's tendrils as they shake in anger.

You ignore all that. "Give me. My memories."

The satrap calms. "You are too impertinent," the mouths around you chorus. "I am near immortal. I know the region the man was in. I will continue hunting for that world, and I will eventually have it. But you..."

The large man crushes the memory box. Hyperdense storage crumples easily under the carbon fibre fingers and steaming coolant bursts from between his knuckles.

Fragments drop to the ground.

You stare at them, lips tight.

"Ah," the satrap sighs all around you. "Now those memories only live inside me. They are once again, unique within flesh. So… if you kneel and behave from now on, I'll tell you all about your life. Every time you complete a task, you will return and bow before me right here, and I will tell you about your life. I will give you your past back. Just hand me the head, and kneel."

"You actually believe that I will hand you this head, and take a knee?" you ask.

"I do. From here, those are your only two choices. So the question is…"

You throw the head aside and hold the machete in both hands firmly.

As expected, half the men and women in thrall scrabble for the head. There's a twinge of regret. Maybe John would have been able to hide in his ship if you hadn't shown up. Maybe he would have been able to sneak enough fuel to his ragged fleet to make for that hidden world.

But you doubt it.

And here you are.

Killing the puppets who are in thrall to the satrap is a thankless task. They are human. Many of them would not have asked for this life. They are people from the home world who fell on hard times, and were given a promise of future wealth in exchange for service. If they live long enough. Others were prepaid: a line of credit, a burst of wealth for a year, and then thrall. Others are criminals, or harvested from debtor's prison. Prisoners of war left over from various conflicts.

The Satrapy is 'civilized.' So it says. It doesn't raid for subjects. They have to, nominally, be beings that have lost their rights. Or agreed to lose them.

Doesn't mean most can't see what thralldom is.

But you kill anyway. Their blood, sliding down the

hydrophobic blade to drench your sleeves. The three nearest, beheaded quickly and cleanly. There's no reason to make them suffer.

You walk through a mist of their jugular blood settling ever so slowly to the ground in the lower gravity. The satrap, realizing what's happening, pulls humans around itself. One of them holds deBrun's head in their arms covetously.

The big guy is the artillery.

He advances, legs thudding, even here. Dust stirs. You walk calmly at him. He swings, a mass-driver, extinction level powered punch that grazes you. Because what you have is speed. Mechanical tendons that trigger and snap you deep into his reach.

Just the whiff of his punch catches you in the ribs, though. They all crack, and alloys underneath are bent out of shape.

Warning glyphs cascade down your field of sight.

You ignore it all to bury your blade deep into the giant's right eye socket, then yank up.

Even as the body falls to the ground, you're facing the satrap once more.

"I've already called my brothers and sisters down on the ground to come for you," it says through the remaining puppets. "You are dead."

"People keep telling me that," you say.

And maybe they're right.

The puppets come at you in a wedge. All seven. It's trying to overwhelm you.

You use the machete to cut through the jungle of flesh, leaving arms and limbs on the ground. And when you stand in front of the satrap, it wriggles back away from you in fear.

"Let me tell you a memory," it begs through speakers, using the machines now that it has been shorn of biological toy things.

"It's too late," you tell it. "I'm dead."

You drive the machete deep. And then you keep pushing until you have to use your fingers to rip it apart.

There's a sense throughout the habitat that something major has shifted. Free humans are bunched together in corners, and others are dazed and wandering around. The rumor is that the satrap has suddenly disappeared, or died. But what if it comes back? What happens when other satraps arrive?

You find the docks and a row of deBrun's crew with guns guarding the lock. They stare at you, and you realize you are still covered in blood and carrying a machete. Everyone on the station has given you a wide, wide berth.

"If you wanted to steal fuel, now's the time," you tell them. "The satrap's not going to be able to stop you. Everyone out there doesn't know what to do."

There are some other alien races sprinkled in throughout the station. But they seem to have locked themselves away, sensing something has gone wrong.

Smart.

"Who did the captain leave in charge, if he died?" you ask. They don't answer, but take you back into the ship, and the first mate comes up.

"You're in charge?" you ask.

"Yes," he nods. "I'm John."

You frown. "He called you Jay on the bridge, when I came out."

The first mate smiles sadly. "John deBrun. The junior John deBrun. Jay because we don't need two Johns on the bridge. Though… I guess that won't happen anymore."

"He gave you the coordinates, in case he was taken."

John's son nods. "You were taken with him, by the satrap? You were there?"

You pause for a moment, trying to find words that suddenly flee you. You change direction. "You have three hours to steal as much fuel as you can before forces from the planet below arrive. We should both be long gone by then. Understand?"

"Three hours isn't long enough."

You shrug. "Take what time you have been given."

"You don't understand, we're taking on extra people. People we didn't plan to take on. That adds to the mass we need to spin up. We have the other ships docking hard, and we're taking refugees from Hope's End. People, who if they stay, will be back in thrall at the end of those few hours. We won't have enough fuel to get where we need to go. Maybe, three quarters of the way?"

And out there in space, you were either there or not. There was no part way. No one was getting out on foot to push a ship. Those are cold calculations. They come with the job of captain. Air. Food. Water. Carbon filters. Fuel.

"Sounds like you need to shut your locks soon," you say. "Or you risk throwing away your father's sacrifice."

"I will not leave them," John says calmly. "He may have been able to. You may. But I will not. We are human beings. We should not leave other human beings behind."

"Then you'd better hope your men hurry on the fuel siphoning."

You have no use for goodbyes. You leave him in his cockpit. But you stand in the corridor by yourself in the quiet. Your legs buckle slightly. A wound? Overtired muscles sizzling from the performance earlier? You lean against the wall and take a deep breath.

When you let go, you stare at the bloody handprint.

You lost it all. So close, and you lost it all.

And now what? What are you?

You'll never have those memories. They aren't you anymore. You are you. What you have right now, is you. What you do next, will be you. What will that be?

A cold heart and a bloody hand. That's what you've been. What you are.

You turn and go back into the cockpit.

"Is the planet real?" you ask. And look John's son for any hint, any sign of a lie. You can see pulse, heat, and microexpressions. Things that help you fight, spot the move. And now, spot intent.

"It's real."

"There is another way," you say.

"And what is that?"

"Take me with you. Get as much fuel as you can, but leave early. Even if it means we only get halfway to where you are going. I killed the satrap, and everything protecting him. And it wasn't the first. When we run out of fuel, we'll dock and I'll rip more fuel out of their alien hands for you. For you. Understand? I can train more like me. When your fleet passes through, those that stand against us will rue it. I will do this because there is a debt here, understand?"

John looks warily at you. "You were with my father. He didn't kill the satrap?"

"There is a debt," you repeat.

"He helped you?"

"Give me weapons. The non-humans on the station, they enjoy a position of power. They have avoided mostly being in thrall, as we are the new species for that. So even though we have time, they will figure out what we are doing and act against us. You'll want me out there, buying you time."

John nods, and reaches out a hand to shake.

You don't take it. You can't take it. Not with his father's blood still on it.

"Weapons," you repeat. "Before your men start dying unnecessarily."

Cycled through the locks, deBrun's men behind you, you walk past the stream of frightened people heading for the ship.

You stand in the large docking bays and survey the battlefield.

This is who you are. This is who you will be. This is who you choose.

A cold heart and bloody hands.

When this is over, when you help deliver them to their new world and repay your debt, you can go home to Earth. Stalk for clues to your past. See if you wander until you find that palm tree on the island you remember.

But for now, you are right here.

Right now.

Waiting for the fight to come to you.

THE LOA

As the island continent Nanagada turned upwards towards the north it looked, on a map, much like the tail of a duck with its head in the water. Here the rusting iron network of the great Triangle Tracks ran from the tiny tip of Nanagada all the way down to many of the Eastern and Western coastal towns.

The descendants of refugees and islanders from an Earth remembered only in the tales of the past, before all such things were lost, labored on, though the new threat of the Azteca coming over the Wicked High Mountains made many nervous.

And Capitol City, where all the tracks started and ended, was a great amphitheatre of rock created by the ancient old-fathers. It rested on the tip of the peninsula, it's harbor safe between the walls that dipped into the furious northern water.

On a small side street, off by an grey cobble-stoned alley between two bright yellow painted warehouses with red shingled roofs, Adamu helped his friend Treo climb out from a manhole.

Adamu's stomach felt like a tight knot from hunger. The smell of baking bread in the distance made him dizzy as they pushed the heavy manhole cover back into place. Adamu walked out onto Main Street.

"Where we going?" Treo asked.

Adamu hated leaving the safety under the manhole. The

sunlight made him blink. A heavy woman with a basket of laundry on her head brushed past.

"Where we going?" Treo asked again.

Adamu was following the smell of fresh bread. He and Treo had found a single soggy paper bill in one of the storm sewers. They had a chance to buy something fresh.

The small shop with the just-baked bread was called 'Loddy's.' Today it smelled of hops bread. The scuffed wooden door dinged as it closed behind them.

Adamu's mouth watered, and he heard Treo's stomach growl. The thin man behind the counter peered down at the two boys.

"What you want?"

Adamu pointed at a piece of hops bread almost as tall as Treo. Green pieces of hops lay scattered all over the top, and the sides of the cloth covering the wicker basket they lay in.

"That bread," Adamu said.

"What money you have?" The man looked suspicious. He looked up and down their raggedy clothes and unkempt hair.

Adamu took the small, carefully folded bill out from his pocket.

"Ain't good."

"What?" Adamu demanded.

The man jabbed his finger at the bill.

"I ain't taking paper. You don't listen around you or anything? The Azteca coming. A whole army marching from over the Wicked High mountains and coming up to Capitol City for we. I only taking coin."

Adamu stared, crushed.

Treo snatched a cinnamon roll from off the counter.

"Hey!"

"Come Adamu, run."

Adamu ran, hitting the door open, not looking back. People

packed the street, surrounding a large carriage. Adamu pushed in between them to disappear.

"It a Loa," someone yelled.

"They moving he to a safer area, away from the city wall. They scared of the Azteca."

Adamu tripped into the street, and looked up at the carriage. The giant mass of jellied flesh shifted and looked down at him. Translucent eyes blinked, and a coil of metallic tentacles recoiled back behind the leather flap hanging from the side of the covered carriage.

Treo grabbed his arm. His fingers were sticky.

"What that?"

"One of their gods," Adamu said.

A priestess stepped protectively forward, and Adamu grabbed Treo's arm. They ran back towards their manhole, to slip under the city and join the other children beneath the streets. Adamu's posse.

Before they slipped back under Adamu took one last look around. These topside people were lucky. He envied them their fresh bread and succulent fruit, their easy lives.

Capitol City's roots lay deep in the solid rock of Nanagada. Honeycombs of sewer systems, access tunnels, and large caverns lay beneath the many streets.

"Easy, man, watch where you going."

Outlets poured waste-water, city water, toiletwater, and excess air back out along the sides of the walls that ran along the ocean. The old-fathers designed this city well. And long after all their powers failed, Capitol City remained.

"I know what I doing."

Adamu held the oars and let his boat glide. He knew the bowels of Capitol City better than the streets. Where the great walls of the city left land and stretched out around the sliver of ocean that was Capitol Harbor, great ten foot high inlets took the Harbor water flowing in from under Grantie's Arch and let it run underneath Capitol City to clean away the trash, silt, and dirty water.

Someone swore. The voice echoed.

"Nothing. My net dry."

The inlets lay under the great piers of the harbor. No one bothered to look between the cracks of old stone steps and the forests of pillars that held the harbor up.

Here all the trash in Capitol Harbor eventually came, and was scavenged. Adamu rowed on, brown water sloshing around the bottom of his slowly leaking boat. Without the trash to recycle and sell, he would have died underneath Capitol City a long time ago.

"How come you ain't bailin'?" Adamu demanded. Treo held his knees up on the rear bench, his feet out of the water sloshing about.

"What? That water nasty."

"Treo. Pick up the bucket and keep we from sinking and swimming in it already."

Treo grabbed the bucket and starting throwing water over the side of the boat. It scraped wood as he dragged the lip over floorboards.

"Okay, stop."

Rusty pitons had been hammered into the pillars, and nets strung across them. Adamu stopped by the net's edge and shipped his oars. The cold water ran down the handles onto his hands.

He leaned over and grasped the top of the net, slippery with mats of algae.

Careful not slice his hands on the white pimply barnacles, Adamu tugged upward. Treo did the same over the back of the boat.

"A fish," Treo said. He used two hands to grab a yellow-tailed snapper and threw it to the bottom of the boat. It flopped weakly in the scummy water.

"Find a few more, get we some lime to soak in, bread it up, that go be a good dinner," Adamu said.

Treo nodded, still holding the top of the net in his hands. Adamu started pulling more net up. The large weights on the other end dragged over the bottom muck. He occasionally draped a section of the net over the oar pegs to hold the net from slipping back over.

He found another few snappers struggling in the net. Bottles floated around, trapped at the top. Adamu stood up and put them in the bin under his seat.

"Uhh," Treo sounded unsure. Then he jumped back from the net. "Ay, what that?" He shouted.

Adamu set the net over an oar peg and stood up.

Pink flesh bumped against the U-shaped transom.

"It a body," Treo said. He ran to the front of the boat, shaking and knocking the oars aside. Adamu leaned over to snag one almost falling into the water.

Adamu shook his head. He'd seen corpses wash up against the nets. A waterlogged body usually turned pale, not pink. Unless someone just threw this one in, it shouldn't be pink.

He looked around nervously. There were no other boats. "Damn."

He took the oar and poked at the pink blob. It rolled over. Translucent eyepatches gleamed back at him.

"It a Loa," Treo said. "Like what we had see up in town."

But Adamu remembered more from his previous live living above on the streets.

"That Loa from the 5th Street temple. I seen him before. He dead." Adamu pushed it out from under the boat further. One of the creature's tapered limbs tore out of the net. It floated free. A ring of metal gleamed around the tip.

Treo stood up on the bow and peeked over the length of the boat, curiosity getting the better of him. "If that a god, how it die?"

"I don't think they really gods." Granny believed the old religion, but not like the Vodun priestesses in the city. She said the Loa were life guides, spirits you called and heard, but didn't see. She called the City Loa 'false abominations.' And until she died,

81

was the only person above who was good to Adamu. He didn't see any reason to disbelieve her.

Treo furrowed his eyebrows.

"You don't believe Voodoo?"

Adamu bit his upper lip.

"It don't matter." He did not want to mess with Treo's head. Better he come up with his own ideas.

He poked at the body again.

If something could kill this, he thought, they might kill us.

Adamu whistled loud for attention.

"Hey, hey. We need clear out."

"What?" The other kids stood up and started complaining.

"Adamu, we ain't finish yet?"

"What wrong man?"

"A Loa dead in the net," Adamu shouted. "Something kill it."

There was quiet. Quiet enough that Adamu heard the faint rustle of something stir above his head. He hadn't looked up the side pillar they floated by.

"Treo!" He shouted, sitting down hard enough to splinter the seat. He grabbed for the extra oar, but missed it. Scrabbling backwards to protect Treo he held the oar in front of him and looked up.

A man held himself up using the high tide piton. He wore a long, heavy overcoat stained with green splotches and dirt. His shoulder length dreadlocks swayed with him as he lowered into the boat. His dusky skin was lighter than any of theirs, but matched his brown eyes perfectly. Adamu could see his muscles even through the big coat.

He squatted on the aft bench. Adamu thrust the oar at him.

"Easy," the man said. His voice, calm, made Adamu swallow. It sounded different, with a strange flat accent.

"Look," Adamu said. "We ain't see nothing, we ain't go tell nothing. Let us go."

The man smiled. He leaned over and looked at the Loa.

"I didn't kill it," he said. "But I know what did." He casually reached a hand over the back and rolled the Loa over. Claw marks furrowed the skin, leaving flaps of flesh dangling from the Loa's torso. White ooze leaked into the water. "Teotl."

Adamu shivered. Mothers scared children inside at night with tales of Azteca human sacrifice and atrocity. The Teotl were the Azteca's gods, like the Capitol City gods, only bloodthirsty beyond imagination.

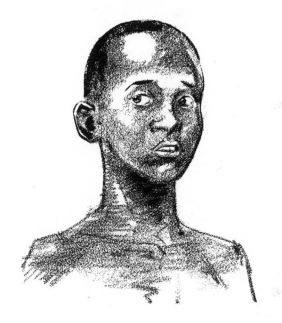

One of the posse's boats rounded the pillar. Tito balanced on the bow with a spear.

"What you name? If you touch any of we I go strike you down," he shouted.

The man looked at Adamu.

"Things real thin for you." He waved at the three gasping fish on the floorboards. He reached in his pocket and set a small piece of gold on the middle seat.

Adamu reached forward and looked at it.

A single gold tooth, a fleck of brown blood still on the root side. He looked up at the man.

"What you name?"

"Pepper."

Adamu put the gold tooth in his pocket.

"What you want?"

Pepper smiled.

"I want you to help me catch the teotl."

Adamu looked the massive man back in the eye.

"How? We small."

Pepper stopped smiling.

"I need you to be my bait," he said.

Treo grabbed Adamu's shirt.

"Don't do it, Adamu," he whispered. "That ain't right."

Pepper patted his pocket.

"I have more gold," he said. "Will you help, or will I find someone else?"

Adamu looked down at the fish in the bottom of the boat.

"No. We helping."

"Good." Pepper looked at the other boat coming towards them. "Who are you?"

"We the posse," Adamu said.

"The posse?" Pepper asked.

"No one care for we," Adamu said. "Or what we name. We just... the posse."

The second boat hit, shaking Adamu. Tito jumped in, his spear aimed straight at Pepper. Pepper yanked it out of Tito's hands and snapped it. He smacked Tito in the sides with the broken ends. Tito dropped to his knees with a cry.

"Don't ever point this thing at me again," Pepper said evenly.

Adamu grabbed Treo's hand and squeezed it. Everything all right, he thought. We just need to stay calm. And take the gold.

The gold would change everything.

Gold tooth in his pocket, nets left behind, Adamu tied up the boat by the edge of the inlet. Pepper got out and stood on the slick stone squares.

He looked out into the dark forest of pillars and the four other boats rowing towards Adamu.

"We will need all your boats," he said. "And your nets. We will sweep the water with them."

Adamu looked around at the posse. They stood with their arms crossed, or leaning back against the sides of their boats. A sullen suspicion of this adult giving them orders sat in the air.

"He paying us in gold," Adamu said, holding out the tooth.

That got attention. They spent their days scrabbling to keep ahead, fishing, scavenging the harbor's garbage. They wore cast offs, torn clothing, brown with years of occasional washings and misuse.

During the rainy season they feared death in suddenly flooded sewers. During dry season they covered their noses with perfume soaked cloths because the left over muck dried up and stank.

How could they pass this up? A chance to end the perpetual stone in the pit of their stomachs?

"What we looking for?" Tito asked. His mouth still remained set, his eyes slit. But gold was gold. He would do what Pepper said.

"A submarine," Pepper said.

"Like the metal one up in the Museum?" Adamu asked. "They dig it out of the harbor. No one know how it work."

"Maybe," Pepper shrugged. "But this one is made of wood."

"Wood?" One of the posse asked.

Pepper nodded.

"What about protection?" Adamu asked. "Them look like sharp claws, whatever rip up that Loa."

A smile.

"The safest place for any of you is right here," Pepper said. He blinked. "Now come, we have to get moving. There isn't much time."

Adamu sent the four boats to pick up the spare nets at pillar
seventeen and twenty. Ten minutes later they had rigged them with
silt weights to drag the bottom.

When he got ready to join one of the boats Pepper put a large
hand on his shoulder.

"We will use your extra boat."

Adamu didn't argue.

Treo stood on the lip of smooth stone, eroded by years of
water rushing up it at full tide, then back out. He shook his head.

"I don't want go," he protested.

"Treo, get in." Adamu didn't want Treo wandering around by
himself, alone, a target for some evil Azteca creature in the dark.

They stepped back in.

As Adamu began to pull on the oars, looking for the best
vantage point to keep the pair of sweepers in sight. And as he did
so, looking around and all the shadows and shapes, a thought
popped into his head.

"Where the Teotl now?" Adamu asked.

"Probably watching us," Pepper said. Treo whimpered.
"Don't worry. It won't do anything yet. Not until we find its
vehicle."

Pepper hunched over in his seat and bundled his long coat
around him. He looked around the boat and began to whistle
quietly to himself.

Adamu bit his lip. Maybe he should have left Treo back there.

After three hours of sweeping Tito got upset and threw down
one of his oars.

"It ain't here," he cried out. "We wasting we time."

Pepper didn't say a word. He took out another gold tooth.
But he didn't give to anyone. He dropped it over the side of the
boat. It plinked into the water and disappeared.

Tito shut up and went back to the oars.

The tension grew as everyone darted glances at the shadows, expecting some monster to leap out over the water towards them at any second. Adamu began to sweat, beads trickling down his spine into the small of his back and lower.

Treo handed Adamu a bottle of water during a break, as the boat coasted forward. Adamu shipped his oars and took the bottle of warm water.

It tasted sweet.

The bowwaves slowly stopped lapping against the hull as the boat lost momentum. Adamu capped the bottle and gave Treo a playful shove.

"Thanks."

He picked the oars back up.

They had found Treo in a drain runoff last year. His ribs showed through his thin skin. Tito said they couldn't just leave him there to die, and Adamu agreed.

Treo's hands had been bound, his wrists bloodied. He'd been beaten severely, lashes running up and down his back and legs.

No one talked about it. Everyone gave up meals to feed him.

Often Adamu sometimes lay awake at night, wondering what right he had to keep Treo down in the sewer.

But he wouldn't allow Treo above. Not until the boy had grown. And even then, Adamu felt nervous about the thought of letting Treo go.

Treo was a good boy. He deserved everything they could give him. And now Adamu saw the gold dancing in front of his eyes.

"Hey!" The shout echoed around them, bouncing around and skimming over the water. Adamu reversed the oars and slowed them down, then turned them around.

"Yeah, yeah, this it."

Tito stood and waved an oar triumphantly. The net wrapped

around a twenty foot long curve of smooth black wood, barely visible as it broke the surface of the water.

Pepper stood up, his coat falling around him. A pair of shotguns peeked out from under the ragged hem. When Pepper looked around them again, his eyes had turned entirely grey, his pupils invisible. Adamu shivered. What magic, or ancient technology, allowed that? He forced himself to keep rowing hard, digging the paddles of the oars into the water to get them to Tito's boat.

And Pepper balanced, hardly swaying as Adamu jerked the boat forward.

Pepper leapt out of the boat and onto the top of the submarine. His boots splashed slightly, and the long submersible rocked.

"This is it," Pepper said. "Now we be careful." He pulled his rifle out from under the long coat. Adamu caught the glimpse of another pistol on his waist,. It had rubber grips.

Looking down from the side Adamu could see not a single joint in the submarine. It looked like it had grown itself out of a single piece of wood, rather than carved or built in any fashion.

Still balancing, Pepper used his free hand to spin the lever on the top. He opened the hatch and looked in quickly, rifle first.

"We should sink it," Adamu said.

Pepper shook his head. He closed the hatch, then stepped back onto their boat.

"I have my own uses for it," he said. "And first we wait for this creature. I wish to know why it is here."

He took out the spare rifle Adamu had seen earlier. Colorful feathers had been glued onto the side, and blocky glyphs of serpents and stick figures carved into the stock.

"That has two shots in it," Pepper said. He handed it to Adamu. "And then you can throw it into the water. Be careful."

Adamu took the rifle and examined it, looking over the gaudy orange painted firing pin, and sighted down the barrel.

"How the Teotl go come for we if he don't have no boat?" Treo asked.

"He'll swim," Pepper said. "Or maybe this one will fly. I don't know."

Adamu looked up at the tops of the pillars.

"How you don't know what the Teotl look like?" He asked.

"They take many different forms," Pepper said. "Have you seen many Loa?"

Adamu slid the oars back between the two pegs. He turned the boat around.

"They hide behind curtains, or shadows. They have holy ones, who tend to them. I saw the 5th Street Loa once," Adamu jerked his head off in the direction where they discovered corpse. "It couldn't walk, or move. It just told people things, and they did what it asked."

Pepper shifted in his seat, the boat swayed slightly.

"They specialize. Different ones do different things. They are born the same, and then spend the rest of their lives changing their bodies towards some function."

"Loa or Tetol?" Adamu asked.

"Both. Azteca, or Capitol City, they are the same thing," Pepper grunted. "Invaders. Dictators. Not human." A distant splash, barely audible, echoed ever so slightly through the pillars. Pepper raised his hand.

It was coming through the water for them.

Adamu shipped the oars quickly and hopped over to stand in front of Treo.

"Get down."

He stood, rifle held awkwardly in front of him. All around the water stayed calm. It made Adamu's pulse flutter, and his body tingle with fear.

The other boats rocked, oars clattering, voices chatting.

"Shhh," Adamu hissed. They fell silent.

Tiny waves lapped against the pillars. The beginning trickle of one of the small city-pipes emptying out near them.

Were was it?

Right there! A shape beneath the water by Tito's boat. Tito screamed and jumped into the water with the broken half of spear at it. He missed. The shape ducked deeper into the water. The boat splintered from beneath, and water splashed out from inside it. Pepper didn't move, but watched, his gun aimed.

"Where it is?" Adamu demanded. His friend floundered in the water and Adamu aimed the gun near him, hoping to catch another glimpse. He held his breath, his hands shaking slightly.

"Row us closer," Pepper ordered. They'd drifted several feet away from the submarine.

Adamu didn't want to move from the bow.

"Now. Quick."

Adamu walked over to the seat, uncocked the rifle, lay it by his feet, and took up the oars. One long single pull shoved the bow against the submarine.

Pepper sniffed the air.

"Watch you-self," he said.

The boat jolted. The planks behind Adamu ripped upon as the Teotl pulled itself aboard. Splinters sprayed onto his neck and down his shirt. Adamu turned around and caught a faceful of salty water, and the glimpse of smooth gray skin.

"Treo!"

Adamu grabbed the gun as fast as he could, swinging it around as Treo began screaming. The Teotl stood still for a second, the fins and slick skin dripping water. It looked almost human.

Then one razor-clawed hand snapped forward in a blink and ripped Treo's neck out in an explosion of blood. It splattered against the insides of the bow and bench.

Adamu closed his eyes and pulled the trigger. The gun did not fire.

Pepper moved forward with inhuman speed and shoved Adamu out of the way. Adamu smacked his head against the side of the boat and toppled into the water. Gasping, dizzied, he hung on with a hand.

Tito tread water not even five feet away, horrified.

"Treo done dead," Tito whimpered.

Adamu closed his eyes and pushed his head against his arm and the boat.

Pepper struggled in the boat over him, rocking it, until the huffs and grunts stopped. A steady mewling began. Adamu let go of the boat and swum away, to join Tito.

They watched Pepper stand up with one of their nets, the Teotl bundled up tightly in it. He picked the package of flesh up, his coat torn, blood and white ooze covering him and limped off Adamu's boat over to the submarine.

He tossed the Teotl inside, then followed it in.

The mewling stopped, and screaming began. Adamu didn't understand the language, but he could hear the pain. Tito threw up in the water around him, and kept pushing the bile away from him.

The screaming continued for almost an hour. Adamu's boat sank. They pulled Treo's torn and bloodied body up onto the submarine and cried together.

"Little brother," Adamu said over the screams, and wrapped his spare shirt around Treo's neck and chest. He held him in his lap. "I'm sorry."

They were tired. They pulled Treo into the one of the two remaining boats and got ready to leave. Gold or not, Adamu didn't care anymore.

The screaming stopped just before they left. Pepper came back up to the top of the wooden submarine. He was not just

covered in blood and Tetol ooze, he stank of it. It made Adamu
sick to his stomach. Pepper crossed onto the boat.

Adamu shook his head and blinked out the tears.

Pepper squatted next to him.

"I'm sorry," he said.

Adamu nodded.

"That how it is, right?" He sniffed. "You didn't shoot that
thing, you wanted it alive. The price of one boy acceptable. You
just like anyone else, we nothing to you."

Pepper didn't reply.

"So now what, Mr. Pepper," Adamu asked. "You go give us
another couple piece of gold, and then you escape in that little
submarine. Right? I hear on the street Azteca coming. You go
make a quick escape?"

And if so, what did Pepper care about them, scrapping
around here. What was another life for what Pepper wanted?
Adamu realized that he hadn't escaped anything by going down
into the sewers.

Pepper took out a small bundle from under his ripped out
coat. Adamu could barely hold it up.

"It's all gold," Pepper said. "Melt it down before anyone sees
what it all is, or they will ask questions and take it from you."

Adamu opened it. A crown with a panther. Jade hammered
into anklets, and wristbands. All Azteca, he recognized.

He looked back at Pepper.

"How you get all this? Who you is really?"

"The Azteca a scary night story, right?" Pepper asked.

Adamu nodded.

"Well I am the Azteca's scary story. I have been that for a
long, long time. They marching toward Capitol City. They will be
here soon." Pepper winked. "Take the gold. I don't need it
anymore," he said. "But don't waste it."

Adamu swallowed.

"I'm sorry for everything," Pepper said. He walked back off
the boat onto the submarine. When he crawled into the hatch he

paused and looked back at Adamu.

"They will need your knowledge of this part of the city, if the Azteca do break the walls," he said. "You can help."

Adamu shook his head.

"No one will come to us and ask."

Pepper stepped further down.

"I hope I never see you again," Adamu said to his face, all that was visible now. He trembled.

Pepper closed the hatch.

They rowed off, watching the submarine sink beneath the waves. They were alone. Adamu slumped against the back of the boat, the bag of treasures in his lap. It was enough, he guessed, to make their fortunes.

In any other manner it would have been an almost magical win. A dream come true.

He picked up the crown and looked at it. Disgusted he threw it over the side and listened to it hit the water with a distant splash.

"No," Tito yelled. He leapt forward and grabbed Adamu in a bearhug. He wrestled the bag away, gold teeth tumbling out into the water washing about Adamu's legs. "It hurt, man. But we need it to survive."

Adamu began to cry again, and Tito held him.

Several days later Adamu stepped into Loddy's. He looked around at the counters, piled high with bunches of green bananas, plaintain, cans of corn, and baskets of bread by the counter.

Adamu picked up a small bag of hard sweets colored yellow and pink pastel. They didn't look all that tasty.

Outside a hissing steamcar full of Mongoose men passed by, the soldiers in gray field garb making sure all remained calm in the face of the impeding threat of Azteca invasion.

The thin grocer leaned over the counter, half covered in the shadows. His arm rested over the brass knobs of the freshly polished cash register.

"Hey, child," he grunted. "You even have money for all you looking at? Or I go have to kick you back out my door."

Adamu bit his lower lip.

He pulled out a gold coin. More than Mr. Loddy would make in a week off his overpriced produce. Adamu held the coin in the palm of his hand.

Then he put it back in his pocket, and set down the bag of sweets.

"Yes, sir," Adamu said. "I have the money."

He walked past the counter and out the door.

Out in the street there was no chatter. People hurried to their destinations, hushed except the clatter of machinery and the snort of horses pulling their carriages. It was the calm before the storm. No one paid Adamu any attention as he snaked towards the nearest alley with a manhole.

Under the city he could still survive. Let the Azteca come. Azteca or not, none would notice Adamu beneath the streets. He would survive, as he always had.

An old man sat against one of the walls watching him as he pulled the heavy round cover up.

"Please," the man asked. "Could you spare?"

The old man looked like an Azteca refugee from over the distant Wicked High mountains that split Nanagada off from the Azteca. His once smooth hair was now straggly.

Adamu took the gold coin from his pocket.

"Here," Adamu said. He took the man's callused outstretched hands in his own and gave him the gold. If Azteca came, this man would have more problems.

"Quetzacoatl bless you," the old man cried.

Adamu walked away and sat down on the manhole's rim. He looked at the worried people passing by on the street. He had once envied them.

"Quetzacoatl bless us indeed," he whispered.

Adamu climbed down the rusted iron ladder, pulled the

manhole cover over with two grating jerks, then dropped to the ground.

The dirty water lapped at his new boots, but didn't soak in. Adamu splashed his way back home under Capitol City.

NECAHUAL

We drop out the wormhole towards a mess of a planet by the ochre light of a dying sun. From the cant of orbit, upside down and even then through virtual portholes we can see tiny spots of white light blossom in the atmosphere.

We're liberators.

Each one of those little blossoms of light is an impact. A chunk of rock with a controller vane on it, predestined for a certain point. It clears out the enemy's ability to hit back above the stratosphere.

I know from past experience that sunsets here on New Anegada won't be the same for a long while. As I a child I'd sat on porches near the coast to watch the magnificent sunsets of my own world for many months after The League came to liberate us.

"Man we're dropping the hammer on this backwater shithole," the man across from me says. His white and blue exoskeleton wraps around his body. He looks like a striped mantis. Right now it's plugged into the convex wall of the pod, charging and keeping him from bouncing around as we skate atmosphere.

A single bead of sweat floats loose from his bulbous nose and hangs in the air between us.

"You know much about the target?"

Everyone wants to know juicy details about them.

"Historical info only," I say. "The Azteca of Mother Earth never even called themselves that. They were the Mexica."

I wonder if the black man caddy cornered to right of me has skin-flauge painted on. Hard to tell under the blue and white he's wearing. It's hard not to look askance at him. No one like him on the home planet. But at least he's human, real human, and The League today will be adding another human planet we're told. If there are any aliens here we'll wipe them out, every last one, like they tried to wipe The League out.

"The warrior priests of Mexica were pretty brutal," I explain. "They used to induce hallucination by piercing their foreskin," all the men wince, "and dragging a knotted rope through the tear until they saw visions."

The woman caddy cornered on my left asks, "What is going to be like when we hit?"

"I got the same report you did."

The large island continent of New Anegada on the planet is also the name of the planet. This is confusing for conversation, but no one had consulted with the original colonists, mainly Caribbean refugees from Mother Earth after some minor alien attack a long time ago. Half the continent is New Anegada, the other half is Azteca. Large mountains split them down the middle.

The entire system got cut off several hundred years ago, a forgotten incident, a sidenote of history. The wormhole that connects New Anegada to the rest of the worlds opens up again several weeks ago and shit hits the fan.

We're ordered out, to make sure The League gets here first to offer these humans membership and the Azteca contingent attacks. Now things are messy.

This is all I know.

All four of us are strapped across from each other in the pod, waiting as the heat builds up, looking past each other.

The virtual panorama on the floor screen flickers off.

The buffeting ceases. We're still alive.

"Hello," says a small voice deep inside my inner ear. It's a dry and bored monotone. "I am riding shotgun for you. Got about a minute and thirteen seconds left until you hit dirt, and congratulations, you have just passed the highest probability zone of being shot down by automated Azteca fire."

Which is why it is just now downloading itself into my armor.

"Name's Tai Thirteen Crimson Velvet. Call me Velvet. Lady on your left is Paige, man across is Steven. On your right is Smith. Smith has augmented ears for deafness. If you get hit by anything with a good electromagnetic pulse, it'll wipe his hearing chips and he'll back to being deaf. Just so you know."

All the information we need comes to us from the Tais. Tactical artificial intelligences. Little cybernetic ghosts. They give us the real orders, the real info, so that if we got into trouble they can scramble, leave, and we won't be the wiser for the big picture.

These are tactics learned from many strange, alien encounters. Ones where they could just suck shit right out of your brain and figure out what the enemy's plans were. Humanity adapted. It adopted alien tactics wholesale right back at them.

"Take a deep breath and close your eyes," the Tai orders. "Time to peel."

The pod explodes. The sides rip back and vaporize themselves. I open my eyes to see the real island of New Anegada directly below me. My heart hammers as we plummet.

The green land rushes faster and faster toward me until the Tai whispers, 'okay' and the chute slides out of the back of my exoskeleton.

There are no explosions, no shots fired at me, just a calm, blue sky and lush green forest below my feet, the rippling blue ocean up ahead. The chute canopy overhead is invisible, and not just on the visible spectrum either.

A minute later my feet hit turf.

I'm on the ground and I have no clue what's going to happen next.

I'm expecting shots. But I only hear wind rustling through palm fronds and the distant foaming sound of waves breaking over reef. I'm expecting Aztec priest-warriors wearing gaudy colored feathers to fan out and attack us. Instead, I'm facing a large three story concrete building painted bright yellow and pink.

It's got terracotta shingling.

I'm expecting anything except a man with his back against a mango tree, chewing a stem of grass, looking straight at me.

"Is this a friendly?" I ask.

"Okay," the Tai says. "Your regular weaponry is locked under my command. You have a tanglegun in your left pocket, if you need to use that. This is a police action, we're not here to kill anyone. There are no hostiles. We're just here to talk and gather information from the locals."

"So this is a friendly?"

"Yes."

I look down. The extendable canon I have aimed at the man is primed, but useless. I let go of the trigger.

"Go ahead," the Tai orders. "We're here to gather information about who the Azteca are, were they came from, and what, if anything, these people can do to help us. I am recording everything back up to HQ. I'll prompt you as needed. If you do this well, you'll be promoted. So will I."

The canon swings back up under my arm to fasten itself to the back of my exoskeleton armor. It's a smooth lubricated slide. A whisper.

The man by the mango tree pulls the stem of grass out of his mouth and stands up.

"So," he says to me. "We been invade or what?"

I have no idea how to respond. I stand there, still, waiting for someone besides me to do something.

"You speak English?" The man asks. He has a deep tan that almost blends into the color of oak and short tightly curled hair. His brown eyes twinkle with a sort of Huckleberry Finn look, but he's wearing a cream colored suit. With no shoes on.

I nod.

"You looking for Bouschulte, right?" He says, the words so quick they blend into each and I stumble over the accent. He ambles over to us.

I spoke my first word.

"What?"

"You. Looking. For. Bouschulte." The man from the mango tree repeats himself as if I'm slow. He looks frustrated for a second. "He up in he house."

"What is..." I swallow, "a bouschulte?"

"It a name. Frederick Bouschulte. If you have a Aztec name like 'Acolmiztli' or some stupidness like that, and you hiding with us, you don't keep calling you-self 'Acolmiztli.' Seen?"

"Seen." I agree out of sheer panic. The Tai in my head is still silent. I wouldn't mind some assistance. The man's accent is hard and I still haven't been given any damn orders.

The man reaches out to touch my face, then stops when I flinch.

"You eye them, chineeman, you do that to fit in with them?"

"It..." was done a long time ago. Far away. "An old tradition my forefathers continued." I'd been too young to protest the removal of my eye folds.

A tiger-striped cat tiptoes out from behind the building and sits down. It starts to lick its tail, working hard at ignoring the five people on the grass before it.

"What you name?"

"Kiyoshi," I say.

"Well, Kiyoshi, let we get on with this so call invasion, eh?"

My Tai must be gone for good, I realize. And looking around at the panicked faces of the three other soldiers I fell out of the sky with, I realize theirs are dead too. We're on our own. Somehow these people can jam the Tais, though I have no idea how.

The panic attack comes and goes swiftly. Old training takes over. Yes the Tais make the decisions, but we have training. We're still soldiers. We're still mobile representatives of The League.

I grab the man's shoulders, tangle gun aimed right dead in the middle of his forehead. At this range the tangle gun is lethal.

"What's going on?" I hiss. "Tell me what is going on!"

He snaps loose of me, shrugging my armored arms aside as if

they were only a nuisance. The motion is quick enough I have trouble following it. There is, surprisingly enough, a small knife now shoved up between the joints in my armor.

Smith aims his tangle gun at us, but it's an empty gesture. Our tais hamstrung us, took away our lethal force. Orders...

"You conquest failing."

"There is no fucking conquest," Steve snaps. "We're here to save you from the Azteca."

"Yeah man, so I hear. But one thing: seeing that we been making do for a few hundred years already you might wonder what we know that you ain't figure out yet. Second thing: you here to tell us what to do, right? Because you assume we don't know what we doing. You want tell us what to do, how to think. That mental conquest friend. Mental."

A boom shakes the air. Paige looks up at the sky. None of us can see anything, but I shiver.

"Any of you able to contact anyone?" Paige asks.

We all try. Shake our heads. We're cut off.

"Come inside with me now," our new host says. "Drop you weapon to the ground. You don't need them."

For some reason, without the tais, the three soldiers are looking at me. Command structure has returned to our small unit. Ironic how we fall into the old patterns. This is what it would have been like in The League before the Xenowars. Only then it wasn't The League, just spacefaring humans associated with their old national origins on the mother planet.

I have a decision to make.

"Do you have any way that we can communicate to our superiors?" I ask.

Jami nods.

"That we do," he says.

Into the rabbit hole I decide, and nod. We drop our tangle guns and the blade near my ribs disappears just as abruptly as it had appeared. I still want to know how it got under my armor.

"The name Jami," the man in the cream suit says, shaking my

hand. "Jami 'Manicou' Derrick."

Jami turns around, and we follow the barefoot, dapper man into the concrete-block house. We troop past the cat, which is now working on cleaning an extended furry back leg.

Jami asks us if we read much. He wants to know about 'War of the Worlds,' an ancient text, he tells us, but with an interesting moral to it.

None of us have read it.

He laughs gently, takes off his tie and suit jacket and hangs them off the back of a canvas chair.

"You'll wish," he laughs at us. "You should have wait and talk with everyone longer. So now, it a mess. The League trying to come in and reshape everything to be just like it wants it, and it ain't that easy."

The door creaks open and we look straight into the face of the enemy.

The Azteca reclines in a leather chair while an elderly black lady in a bright red and yellow patterned shawl carefully snips at his flat hair. A red cape drapes around his knees where his hands rest, gently crossed over each other. The gold plug in his nose glints in the light streaming through a large opened window, and his jade earrings dangle as he slightly turns his head to regard us.

Blue eye shadow swirls around the crow's feet that crinkle the edges of his eyes. His black smeared lips twitch.

"The League has arrived," he pronounces, looking at our uniforms. "What do you think of our conquerors, Jami?" Jami is leaning against the concrete wall, arms folded, looking at the small ensemble in the room.

"The first conqueror of Tenochtitlan arrive in small numbers,"

Jami said. "They had armor and superior technology. The League only got the large number and the armor."

Jami smiles sadly at us.

"But this is not a group of Spaniards with gold lust and domination in their hearts," The Azteca says. "The League is here to save us. Is it not?"

His eyes are piercing. Something has wounded him. He hates us.

"The first conquistadors thought they were saving the savages back then too," he adds.

I have nothing to say, but stand straight and return his restrained fury with a calm gaze of my own. I am a professional.

"You done, then, Frederick?"

"I miss my true name."

Jami sighs.

"I guess it don't make no difference what you call yourself now."

Acolmiztli stands up and gathers up the cherry bowl with his hair clippings in it.

"I'm not much of a believer," he says, "but the old ways are specific. You must have your hair cut in a way that does not lose *tonalli*. Or you risk losing the strength of your spirit." He takes a deep breath. "In times like these, I need all the strength I can get."

The door slams behind him.

"He's bitter," Paige notes. They've been taking my lead, remaining quiet. I'm in charge. I'm their tai.

"The League should look very very carefully into assuming," Jami says, looking at the door with us, "that all Azteca same."

There are, he tells us, Tolteca. Reformed Azteca who have spurned human sacrifice and made great changes to Azteca society in the last hundred years.

My stomach flip flops.

"Human sacrifice?"

Jami unfolds his arms.

"Acolmiztli tells me he only sacrificed snake, bird, and

butterfly. He say," and Jami imitates Acolmiztli's voice perfectly...
"Because he so loved man Quetzalcoatl allowed only the sacrifice
of snakes, birds, and butterflies. As he was opposed to the sacrifice
of human flesh the three sorcerers of Tula drove him out of the
city. The people of Tenochtitlan did not follow Quetzalcoatl.
Instead, they followed the war-god Huitzilopochtli or Xipe-Totec:
the flayed god. Then the fifth sun was destroyed and we lived in
the sixth and it became a time of change."

It sends shivers down the back of my spine.

"You said you had communications equipment," I fold my
arms. The shivering continues. "We'd like to use it now."

I shiver again, my knees weak. Jami catches me under my
arms as I drop to my knees.

"What's happening?" I'm disoriented; the walls of the room
seem to bend in on themselves.

"Remember how I tell you you should have read Wells?" Jami
says. "Come on." He helps me over to a wooden bench and opens
a cupboard. I vaguely recognize the device behind the wooden
doors. It looks like a museum piece. But it responds to a wave of
my hand and my voice.

Static is my only reply. There is accusation in my angry stare,
but Jami gestures at the device.

"Try again. You feeling rough."

Sweet drips from my forehead, the shivers continue wracking
my body. This time I find a carrier signal and send a voice request
up. Archaic. But they reply.

"Who is this? Identify."

I do, giving personal ID codes and answering questions until
the voice on the other side is satisfied.

"We give nothing away by saying we're doing a retreat," it
says. "All ground assaults have been infected with some sort of
virus, we're losing this battle. We have your touchdown
coordinates. Be outside in five minutes for a starhook. You'll be in
quarantine upon return."

Then it's gone.

My three companions are sweating and sprawled on the floor. Infected. Quarantine.

"When we saw you," I say. "You walked over to us, touched me," my hands go up to my face.

"Acolmiztli gave it to me, and I passed it to you," Jami says.

"Is it fatal?" I ask Jami.

He shrugs.

"Better get back up to orbit and find out, right? I look alright, but I could have antidote." He smiles.

I purse my lips.

"Get up," I order everyone. It has been an interesting being in charge. I'm glad to see the end of it coming. Paige, Smith, and Steve struggle up. Smith leans heavily on Steve. "Get outside, now."

We're a pathetic group that pushes through the door with Jami following us. My knees wobble, but I manage a convincing stride through what looks like a bar.

Dim lights cast shadows, and from those shadows loom wooden tables where several men in khaki camouflage toast us with their glasses and sly grins. I see no weapons, but now I wonder if their weapon isn't the fever raging inside of me.

My gut spasms. The pain almost blinds me.

"Come on." I push my three soldiers on in front of, shoving my hand against their hard armor, ignoring an unidentifiable chuckle from somewhere in the room.

But halfway through the room text scrolls over my vision. My own implants are failing, no longer able to heal my body or regulate it. I'm nothing more than flesh right now. I have no soldier-sharp senses, no wired edge for combat.

I trip over a chair, grab the table to steady myself, and when I blink everything is clear.

Right before me is a large aquarium. Something sinuously moves through the tank and presses against the glass. I stumble closer and a woman stares right back at me through the refracted water and solid glass with wide brown eyes. Sheets of her oak-colored hair twirl behind her head. Her super pale skin has an almost greenish tint.

The eyes hold me until my face presses right against the glass. "Beautiful, isn't she."

Acolmiztli grabs my shoulder.

"She was a present. From one of my brothers. A gift from the Emporer Moctezuma the Ninth."

Her smooth stomach fades into the singular muscle and pilot fins of her tail's trunk. The wide fins are splayed out. They're delicate, yet powerful enough to drive all six feet of her through the water with a flick.

Which she does. Out away from the glass.

Then she turns back, looks at me, and her hands flutter.

It's too hallucinogenic. I walk away from the tank.

"Keep moving damnit." Smith looks at me, face blank. He doesn't understand a word.

His hearing implants have all failed.

But we're moving, and out the door into the sunlight. I lean back and look into the sky. Nothing yet.

"Why are you doing this to us?" I ask Jami, who is still right behind us.

"The Azteca doing it to you."

"But you knew about it," I snap.

"Yes."

"And yet you did nothing. You collaborate with them."

"You the one that drop out the sky and land. We didn't force you."

Overhead I hear a roar, then a rumble.

"But all those deaths..."

"All because of you. Consider: before you came we were changing the Azteca from the bottom up, and inside out. The Azteca a hornet's nest, and we blow some sweet smoke their way. Now you throwing rocks."

Thunder rolls and a small oval speck drops down out of the sky. The long carbon filament trailing behind it is strong enough to reel us all up from the ground we're standing on into orbit and then into hold of a waiting mothership.

"Snap in when it drops," I order everyone. But I turn and look at Jami.

The pod slows to a halt and falls into our midst. Smith walks over and snaps on. Paige does the same, and Steve looks at me follows suit. Three soldiers, ready to get lifted, the cable rising up from between them to rise into the heavens.

"We have a minute, maybe two," Steve says to me.

I'm still staring at Jami.

"Just because you can't spot the power we wield don't mean we defenseless." He stares right back. "We study you. You machines run everything, solider-man. When the conflict came you choose to wipe out the alien threat you faced. And now you all still working on purifying The League. Only human."

"There was no other choice," I say. "When the killing started, we realized it was us or them. Damnit, I was four. You can't hold me responsible. It's different now."

"You kill millions of aliens, we hear. Deport the rest. Cleanse any human not pure human, that tamper with they DNA. You almost wipe yourselves out. Yet you come here to tell us what to do? That's hypocritical."

"We'd never survived if it wasn't for adopting the tais, like they did. We could never have matched their superior military skill." And, despite the fever, I have a trump. "You talk hypocritical. Hypocritical is the mermaid," I hiss. "You let that Azteca keep his slave in his tank. How dirty does that make you?"

I might as well have struck Jami.

"The line is tightening," Steve yells at me.

"You do not give natural rights to any clone in The League?" Jami says. "Any robot? The tais? Artificial people? Because even you wouldn't grant the person in that tank her life. Why the high ground now?"

I walk towards the pod. In a second I'll be yanked out of here into the stratosphere, my suit bubbling out to enclose and protect me. Back to the warrens inside the depths of a troop ship.

"We ain't ignorant," Jami said. "We couldn't make do with metal tech. When the wormhole closed, it was just us and the alien who stayed behind used a different kind of tech. If there is one thing we're good at, it's taking things and adapting them. All my ancestors got handed the trash of the more advanced. Technological hand me downs. Less than perfect trade agreements. Yeah, physical domination gone, but economic and political domination follow. So when we came from the islands to here, we say, never again.

"But then came the aliens, and they created the Azteca to destroy us. We had to make do, take these things and mash them up and sent back up as something unique to us. But now you here. You League would destroy either of us for figuring out how to work with the alien. We need to be cleanse, right? You a superior force, with bigger guns. So we have something you didn't expect. The only way you can find out how to deal with this is talk to us. That's why the Azteca give us the antidote."

They want to 'mash me up,' take me and make me their own and spit me back out to see what changes. They want to figure out how best to handle the new situation that just opened up in their backyard. And I'm a key to a puzzle for them.

I remember a small biological part of what being human is. The reason we fear the Ais, the alien, death, and why The League fights so hard and maniacally against *everything*.

Survival.

Smith's ears are broken, I realize as he signs something at me. A hand flutter, like that of the woman in the tank.

I turn to Jami.

"Okay," I tell him. "I want the same antidote you have, okay?" Jami nods.

"The very same. I promise you."

Paige recognizes what is happening.

"You can't desert," she shouts. "They'll deactivate you."

The rest of the objection is lost. The starhook goes taught and all three of them lift of the ground and accelerate towards space.

I drop to my hands and knees and puke. Tiny pieces of machinery I didn't even know were in me litter the grass with the remains of pasty meals from the last day of eating.

With a deep breath I stand back up.

Jami helps steady me.

"But I have a condition," he says. "You have to help me free her." He's talking about the lady in the aquarium. She's been in the bar for weeks, he tells me, as he helps me back across the lawn. Ever since The League began its bombardment and invasion. Acolmiztli took her here with him, and he won't let her go.

Jami can't free her. His people are helping the Azteca change themselves, but if he were to set the modified woman free, Acolmiztli would blame him. But a rogue League solider with a soft heart, a human heart, could do it.

The Nanagadan's are setting the Azteca against The League. But some Azteca are actually Tolteca, good reformed Azteca. And they are here, but not too reformed. And Jami needs me for a sort of cultural remix experiment, and all I can think of are those almond eyes that plead with me, and the fluttering hands.

"Oh shit," I say, looking up at the sky. The lady in the tank is using sign language. Her hands had moved like Smith's.

And Smith is gone.

I at least want to talk to her.

"Just give me the antidote, please," I tell Jami.

Acolmiztli regards me with suspicion.

"He is back?"

"He a smart man," Jami says, his voice soft and guarded. "He know if a battle turn."

The Azteca laughs, then folds his arms and glares at the men around him.

"Then soon I'll be going home."

"Lucky us."

"The antidote?" I ask Jami. "Where is it?" I'm scared of another attack, of puking something really important out.

"The antidote," Acolmiztli says. "Come on Jami. Can't you give this poor man the antidote? Doesn't he know the antidote is?" Acolmiztli laughs at me and the sound makes me clench my hands. "All those nasty little metal bits inside that talk to each other and to your ships, all those little ghosts running around inside your heads, those intelligent machines, they're all dead. But you'll live. Oh yes, you're just fine. Just like Jami here."

I'll live. Here. But despite Acolmiztli's light tone I know what the result in space will be. All those battle formations, swarming back through the wormhole in retreat, their bows milliseconds away from each other.

Collided and destroyed.

Mass confusions. Systems failures. Those people up there were sitting ducks. No doubt the Azteca's own ships would savage them.

"There is a story I tell, that my father told, and his father before him," Acolmiztli says. Reflections from the wall of water behind me dapple the wall in front of me. "Horse and Stag came into quarreling once, long ago, and Horse went to a Hunter for help in taking his revenge against Stag. Hunter said, yes, but only if you let me put this piece of iron in your mouth that I may guide you with these pieces of rope. And only if you let me put this saddle on your back that I may sit on you while I help you hunt Stag. The horse agreed and together they hunted down the Stag. After this, the horse thanked the Hunter, and asked him to remove those things from him. But Hunter laughed and tied him to a tree, then sat down and had himself a very good meal of Stag. You see what I am saying?" Acolmiztli looks at me.

"No, what are saying?"

The half grin on his lips flitters away.

"Who's riding whom here?"

Jami has sat near me, but at an angle so he can look at both of us.

"You drunk," Jami says.

"Do either of you realize how many people are going to die today?" I yell. I'm shaking angry with everyone. Convinced I was here to land and perform a duty under the Tai's direction, stripped of that leadership, then told I was infected. I had thought I would die, but now I'm alive. I'm a mess.

"Yes," Acolmiztli says. "Can I go watch?" He stands up and totters out of the room.

Jami leans forward and grabs my forearm.

"Please," he hisses.

I turn and look at the lady in the tank, who is staring back at me.

Jami is a man who stared at us when we dropped from space and aimed weapons at him. He slid the machete under my armor and moved quicker than my own machine-aided senses could adjust for. Why was *he* not doing this?

"Who is Acolmiztli really?" I ask.

"The Emperor of the Azteca brother," Jami says. "Here in case the Emperor get attack by you League. Now that the League falling, I imagine he go leave soon."

I swallow.

"Okay."

I know no sign language. I stand in front of the tank and wonder what will happen when I try to take her out.

"And," I whisper to myself, "how do I make you understand that I'm going to help you out. Set you free." There is an ocean nearby, and a small beach that Jami tells me is easy to get to. There is a dirt road that leads from this place straight to it.

"Will you even want to be free?" For all I know she has been in a watery cage like this for all her life. She might only be able to conceive of this being her world. Would it be right to set her free?

And if I do, am I not making enemies with the most powerful Azteca? I've seen what they can do. Can the Nanagadan's do anything to protect me? I doubt it, but they've survived so far.

Sound shakes me free. The pane of glass in front of her is covered in mud and silt and she writes something with her index finger.

READ LIPS.

And on the next line.

TAKE ME AWAY.

This is the right thing to do.

Through a gap in the silt on the glass I tap to get her attention.

"Get back."

I'm still wearing exoskeleton armor, and the helmet section slides up with a quick slap of my palm. The glass shards that hit me when I fire the tangle gun at point black don't slice me to shreds.

The lukewarm water and silt, however, drench me.

She weighs more than I thought, or I'm weak. Her mossy hair drapes over my shoulder. The smell of seaweed fills the room. I stumble over broken glass with her in my arms and get her into a cart filled with water that Jami left outside for me.

Then the pushing run towards the beach, water slopping out over the sides.

Occasionally she pokes her head out of the draining water and stares at me.

Palm trees rustle and shake. My feet crunch on dirt. A dog barks.

The trail turns down. The beach isn't far. I can hear the rhythmic surf and the wind starts to lift sand into the air and into my eyes.

At the end of the trail I pick her up again, lift her out of the cart and run over the sand, almost tripping, until I'm wading into the salty water. She wriggles free of me.

For a second we stare at each other, then she's gone, a shadow beneath the waves. Was there gratitude. I don't know.

It isn't important. I did what I did.

I strip of the exoskeleton, piece by piece, and throw the useless carcass out into the waves.

Overhead the rumble of engines make me to look up and see a machine climbing into the sky from the house. It is gaudily painted, much like I would expect and Azteca flyer to be. It speeds off into the distance like an angry mosquito.

Jami hands me a towel and a drink when I walk through the door. He sits down at a wooden table and just looks at me.

"She leave?" he asks.

"Yes." I nod slowly.

"You'd hope she would stay?"

"I don't know. It doesn't matter. It's done. Acolmiztli?"

Jami smiles.

"He's gone back to his brother."

I take a deep breath and put my hands on the table.

"What am I going to do now?" I ask Jami.

He grabs my hands.

"That one small act of liberation," he tells me, "that little bit of freedom you got her, will have more of an impact than all you ship, you missile, and all you soldier. Understand?"

No, I didn't.

"That lady, her name Necahual. It mean 'survivor.' All this time she been surviving, but that ain't good enough. Now she can have a whole coast, where fishermen will know to feed her. Until she can recover. Because surviving not enough. You can't just survive, Kiyoshi. You must do better than that. And right now The League just surviving. Like you.

"So you just the beginning. The League, we have a lot to offer them too. Along with the Azteca. How to accommodate and incorporate. We been learning how to do this since Mother Earth when were all islanders." He slaps the table. "And we get better and better. Most places, always they get caught up in ruling, dominating, becoming greater, and then falling apart." Jami leans forward. "We learn how to stay outside that, man. It ain't easy," he says. "Always a struggle. But for a much greater good."

I pull my hands free.

"So what do I do right now?" I ask. "How do we start all this?"

Jami leans back in his chair.

"For now, just to talk to me, man. Don't look for information, or try to resolve anything, or figure it all out. Just talk."

I relax a bit.

"And tomorrow?"

Jami smiles.

"There's going to be a lot of work tomorrow. A whole lot of it. We go be very busy."

There is one last thing.

"And the aliens you talked about?"

"I'm looking right at you," Jami laughs.

I freeze my face. I'm nervous about this. All my life I've been scared of them, fighting them, forcing them out of The League.

"Tomorrow," Jami says. "One step at a time, we show you how."

I breathe again. Slowly, savoring the air.

It's more than just surviving. It's living. And I like it.

PLACA DEL FUEGO

Tiago would normally have taken his cut of the picked pockets and stopped right here at the Seaside Plaza. On the very edge, past the vendors on the cobblestone sea walk, Tiago would sit with his legs over the rocky sea wall and look out over the harbor.

Today he only detoured through the plaza to throw the crowd in between him and the woman chasing him.

He'd gotten a brief glimpse of her before the running started: tall, dark eyes, dark skin, dark leather jacket and microfibre pants, careful dreadlocks pulled back into a pony tail.

She was fast in the crowd. She wasn't dodging around legs, using the ebb and flow of the masses to see open routes like Tiago. No, people who got in her way were just...thrown out of the way.

Too strong. She was some sort of soldier, Tiago thought, refocusing ahead.

He might have gotten himself into a bit of a situation.

Slipping onto the seawall path, he sprinted harder, deciding that she was covering the gap in the crowd. To his right the harbor was filled with ships and their cargo, anchored and waiting for a spot to clear on the docks. One of them was throwing out a parasail, the windfoil bucking in the inconsistant harbor wind, but then filling out, rising up into the air hundreds of feet overhead, and then some.

The ship began to pick its way out of the harbor, headed between the tall forest of wind turbines at the harbor's edge: a dangerous move to unleash a windfoil in the harbor, but suddenly Tiago noticed other ships unfurling sails in haste. A cloud of brightly colored parafoils leapt to the harbor sky like butterflies swarming from a shaken limb.

This was worrying enough that Tiago slowed, somewhat, and looked to his left. The warehouses, three and four stories tall, dominated the first row of buildings. But behind them, climbing tenaciously up the side of the mountain, homes and houses colorfully dotted the slopes.

A large, dark mass of gray haze topped the rocky crest and slowly fell down toward the harbor like a heavy cloud.

"Oh shit." Tiago stopped. People in the Plaza were turning too, and murmuring started to spread. They stood up from picnics or meals and the edges of the crowd were already leaving.

The woman smacked into Tiago and grabbed his upper arm.

"Take your damn money," Tiago shouted. I don't want it. I'm sorry. Just let me go."

She looked puzzled as he shoved the paper money into the pockets of her jacket. He may have even given her more than he'd stolen, he wasn't sure.

"What's..."

Tiago pointed up the mountain. "It's going to rain."

She looked over the buildings and let him go. "I forgot."

Forgot? There were two things on the island to remember: stay out of the rain, and avoid the Doacq's attention by staying inside at night.

He bolted. The last thing he saw was the armada of harbor ships, parafoils all full overhead, pulling their hulls up onto their hydrofoil skids as they all scattered to get well clear of the island.

Then the sirens began to wail all throughout Placa del Fuego, alerting its citizens to the descending danger.

From the open sweep of the docks and seawall of the harbor, Tiago headed into the heart of Harbortown. He could breathe easier seeing overhangs above him, and walls he could put his back to.

People hurried about with carbon-fiber or steel umbrellas. Some had already gotten into their hazmat gear.

The klaxons wailed in the background, constantly blearing out their call for all to find shelter. Shops slammed thick windows shut and bolted them, while people yanked tables and chairs and billboards inside. Customers packed in, shoulder to shoulder.

No self respecting shop would let Tiago inside: he was an urchin. His clothes were ripped and melted, his face dirty, and he ran on bare feet.

They'd toss him out on his ass faster than he could get inside.

A faint stinging mist started to fill the air. Tiago squinted and slowed down. The unfamiliar would run faster, but then they'd inhale more. He cupped his hands over his mouth, a piece of flannel in between his fingers to filter the air. He looked down at the cobblestoned street to protect his eyes.

His calloused, flattened feet knew the street. Knew how many steps it would take to reach the alley, knew how many times he'd have to pull himself up on the old pipe running outside to get up onto the roof, and how many more steps across the concrete to get to his niche.

It was a spot between two old storage buildings a few streets back from the waterfront, almost near the Xeno-town enclave. One of them had a large, reinforced concrete gutter along its edge, and when the second building had been built right along side, wall to wall, had left a sheltered ledge the length of the building.

You wouldn't know it to look at it. Twenty street kids had taken bricks and concrete and built a wall along the overhang, blending it into the architecture. It was behind this that Tiago had his very own room.

To get to it, he stepped out over the edge of the building, and behind the wall.

Safe.

His skin stung from contact with the mist, but he could sit in the entryway along the corridor leading down to the seven foot by four foot concrete cubicles they called home, and watch the rain.

It was a floating, frothy jelly, spit out from the trees on the island into the air, that slowly floated down. In most cases it just slowly burned at whatever it landed on, like some sort of an acid.

But after that, all it took was a spark for it to ignite.

In the distance the harbor pumps thrummed to life. All over the city the engineers were fighting back the rain with a mist of their own, taken from the harbor water to coat and rinse the harbor.

Usually being on this side of the mountain protected them. But sometimes the wind changed. Sometimes the fire forests were unusually active.

Either way, you didn't want to be outside. The burns and scars on the children huddled around the openings of their sanctuary testified to that.

The steady rain continued, sizzling as it hit the ground outside.

Tiago relaxed in the quiet among his neighbours as the city fought the rain. He could worry about explaining to Kay why he was coming back with no money from the morning's work later, as much as that scared him. For now, he was just happy to be out of the rain.

He just about leapt out of skin as the wall next to him crumpled and the woman who'd been chasing him shoved her way through and crouched in front of him.

"Hello," she said. "We still have business to finish."

Tiago jumped up to run and the other kids moved back away from him.

But where could he go with the rain coming down so hard?

He looked back at his pursuer. The rain had eaten away at the skin on her forearms, exposing silvery metal underneath. Metal pistons snicked as she flexed her fingers.

A cyborg. Here on Placa del Fuego.

Impossible.

There was no advanced machinery on Placa del Fuego. It all failed on the island, until one reached three miles offshore. In Harbortown the sailors said scientists from other worlds clustered aboard large ships near the wormholes, monitoring what islanders called the deadzone and they called 'an unexplained continuous EMP event.' They claimed the epicenter was somewhere deep under the crust of the planet, right under Placa del Fuego.

The wormholes that lead from the ocean around Place Del Fuego to the oceans of other worlds light years away were anchored in the water just on the edge of the deadzone, and the scientists were there to order the wormholes moved as the deadzone expanded slightly each month.

One street rumor said that one of the alien races had buried a device under the island, intending to use it as a cover for a last stand during the human war for independence. Some said it was the Doacq that bought the deadzone with it.

It didn't matter what or who caused it. The end effect was that the town used pneumatic tubes to send messages. Ox-men from Okur pulled rickshaws around, or people used the compressed air powered trolley cars. Everything ran on compressed air: the town's reservoirs were filled by the myraid wind turbines that festooned the harbor entrance and the exposed ridges of the mountain.

But because of the deadzone, this woman shouldn't have been here, Tiago thought. She shouldn't even work. But in the cramped darkness of his room the cyborg woman squatted on Tiago's handcarved wooden stool.

As Tiago turned on a bright white LED lamp she counted off a lot more money than he'd stolen, or given back to her. Bill after bill after bill. A massive fistful. A month's takings.

It hovered between them.

"Before you tagged me and made the pick," she said, "you seemed to know your way around the harbor. I need someone like you."

Tiago took a deep breath. He wasn't sure if he needed someone like her.

She was trouble.

The hesitation must have been obvious to her. She smiled. "I'll double what you want."

What was the alternative? Tiago took the money. He'd be a fool not to.

"What are you looking to do?" he asked.

"I need to find the person at the top of the underground. Who sees all and knows all." The cyborg shifted, and the stool creaked. Tiago grimaced. It was made of imported wood, and it was his most precious posession. "I'm looking for Kay."

"Kay?" Tiago feigned confusion.

"You know who I'm talking about," the woman smiled.

He did. He wasn't very good at lying straight-faced. He swallowed nervously. "What do you need from her?"

"I need Kay's help." Tiago waited for more, and the cyborg continued. "To find my grandfather. How do I find this person?"

"You don't find Kay," Tiago said. He folded the money away into the depths of his ragged clothes. "She finds you. Go find yourself a nice room along the waterfront somewhere. Kay will show up now that someone knows you're trying to find her. That's how it works."

"Word on the street." The woman leaned forward and held out her hand. A card rested in her palm. "I'll pay you the other half when I meet Kay. Come find me tomorrow at noon."

Tiago took the card. An address had been scribbled onto it. "What is your name, then?"

"Nashara."

Nashara. A cyborg called Nashara. The Nashara? Was he really talking to a living, breathing legend?

Tiago's hands shook.

She was a lot more than just trouble.

He'd gotten himself in way, way deep into something.

Nashara, left, walking out in to the sizzling rain like it was no more than an inconvenience.

It was only a moment before Tiago's neighbours parted and the tiny figure of Kay walked out. Her grey eyes took in the broken brick with a flick before she turned to face him. Her hair was cut just short of her ears, almost boyish. She was shorter than Tiago, something that always surprised him. In his own mind she stood much taller. "I'll have it repaired," she said calmly, flicking her head at the destruction.

Kay's fixing the damage would obligate them to her.

But no one said anything. Refusing it would be an even bigger problem.

They might come to beat him up tonight, Tiago thought. If they weren't too scared.

"You were here the whole time?" Tiago asked, his voice cracking slightly with fear.

Kay ignored his surprise. "That was a Nashara. Here on the island. I wonder how she's able to work here?" Ox-men: two large slabs of hairy muscle, large eyes and flat noses, squeezed into the passageway behind her, stooping over to fit. They regarded Tiago with dull, incurious eyes.

"I don't know..." Tiago muttered.

Kay unpacked a kevlar poncho and pulled it carefully on. She buckled on a gas mask. Behind her, the two Ox-men did the same.

In a muffled voice she told Tiago, "Do you know how expensive it would be to shield someone like her, a cyborg, to be able to function in the deadzone? That must be what she's done. It means she has access to...incredible resources." She paused thoughtfully, thinking about that. Then she continued. "I have preparations to make before I'll meet her. Keep your appointment. I'll send someone for you both."

She stepped out into the rain, and the Ox-men followed her. The three of them disappeared over the side of the building in the haze, and Tiago turned around to face the boys trying to hide in the shadows.

He could tell by the fear on their faces that they would not be bothering him.

They were far, far too scared of Kay.

So was he.

Nashara sat at a table outside a seawall restaurant, surveying the Plaza over a cup of tea. A few small fires had broken out the night before where jellied rain had landed on canopies or abandoned stalls. But considering the strength of last night's storm, it wasn't too bad, Tiago thought. He'd certainly seen worse.

His new benefactor motioned Tiago to sit with her.

"It's odd," she muttered as he sat. "All this stone, brick, slate. Leather for clothes. No wood, no fabrics. Hardly any trees, not even scrub. Grim."

Tiago looked down at his patched clothes. She was surprisingly ignorant about the island if she was the real Nashara. The real Nashara had cloned her own mind to infect alien starships in the fight for human independence. The real Nashara was a founder of the Xenowealth. The real Nashara was a force of nature. That Nashara, it seemed to Tiago, would, at least know about stuff here on the island. "Rich people have them," he said. "In those glass houses."

"Greenhouses?"

Tiago shrugged. "Sure."

Sometimes, in the quieter moments, looking out over the harbor, he'd wondered what the places were like out over the horizon, and through the wormhole the ships sailed through to get to the oceans of other worlds, and through wormholes in those oceans to even more. Other worlds where things were made, and then transported here. Where people like Nashara came from.

But it was useless to daydream too much about where the ships went. Because they weren't taking Tiago along with them. No matter how much he wished for it whenever he sat on the sea wall.

Nashara set her tiny wooden cup down and stood up. "I think Kay will be receiving us now."

Tiago turned around, and the two Ox-men he'd seen last night had silently, amazingly for their bulk, walked up right behind him.

They didn't have to say anything, they turned around and began to walk away. Nashara followed.

And that, he thought, was the end of that.

Only it wasn't.

Up at the end of Onyx street, down the stairs cut into the side of the road and in the basement of an old house tunelled into a rock outcropping at the very edge of town, was one of Kay's many lairs.

He'd been summoned there, two days later.

Amber late-afternoon light pierced the dusty windows, and a menagerie of Placa del Fuego's shadowy denizens milled about. There were more Ox-men, some Runners, and even a few simple-minded Servants. Lots of grubby kids like Tiago, many of them faces he recognized from Elizan's crew crowded in, as well as others from all over the rest of the city. They were Kay's crew, now, all of them. She owned the Waterfront and the Back Ring, and was almost done finishing up controlling the Harbor.

If it was criminal, and happened in Placa del Fuego, Kay wanted to run it.

It had been different, last year. Last year Tiago worked for Elizan; a high strung old man who would leap at a chance to whip anyone who'd held back the take.

A tough life: Tiago still had misshapen broken bones to prove it, but it beat trying to live outside alone. Something he'd learned quickly enough.

Placa del Fuego had no heart for the homeless.

When Kay appeared on the streets in the Back Ring, rain-burned and tired, she'd been ignored. For the first week. The second week she'd figured out the command structure of one of the drug cartels and executed the commander with a sliver of knapped flint.

Within days the cartel danced to her tune.

Rumors said she came from Okur, where the birdlike alien Nesaru had established a colony. Under the Bacigalupi Doctrine, anticipating the lack of fuel and the collapse of the interstellar travel after the war for independence, the Nesaru had bred humans into a variety of forms to serve them. Nesaru engineered, bred, and reshaped human Ox-men and Runners had fled Okur to Placa del Fuego. So had Kay.

She was something else, Okur refugees said. Something designed to control the modified human slaves under the Nesaru's thumb. She could read your thoughts by the slightest change in your posture, a twitch in a facial muscle. She emitted pheremones to calm you, convince you, and used her body to control your personal space.

You were a computer, waiting to be programmed. She was your taskmaster. A perfect, bred, engineered, manipulator of humankind.

"Tiago," Kay said, beckoning him closer. "Nashara and I have quite a job for you."

Nashara stepped out from behind a thick stone pillar. "There will be considerably more money in it for you."

Kay put a protective arm around Tiago. "I really need your help with this, Tiago."

He stiffened slightly as she moved in closer, creating a tiny world between just the three of them. "What do you need?" he asked, hesitant.

"You keep a low profile, Tiago. Back of the crowd. You don't try to cheat me of my cut. You wouldn't even dare think of it."

Tiago nodded. Don't get noticed. Don't cross dangerous people like Kay unless you could run. Melt into the background. These were core life principles of his. It was why he made a good pickpocket. There was even a mid-sized bounty available for his capture.

"More importantly, you've been in the Dekkan Holding Center," Nashara said. In the distant background the sound of rain alarms drifted through the streets. A night storm. The worst kind.

A cold chill gripped Tiago. "You want me to go back to The Center?" Images of the dark warrens flitted back to the front of his mind.

"Not as such." Kay pointed a kevlar poncho and gas mask

hanging by the door. "Suit up."

They walked through the slowly darkening streets, the rain hissing against their protective gear. Nashara wore goggles and a long leather fisherman's coat that seemed impervious to the rain, Kay the same outfit as Tiago.

Their footsteps clicked against cobblestone as Kay led them through sidealleys and tiny backstreets so cramped they had to move through them single file.

No one else was out.

Tiago stopped a tremble in his hands at the thought of being out at night.

Several times they came to dead ends, where small locked doors stopped Kay's progress. But a few knocks in a pattern and they would open, and the trio would tromp through someone's front room, leaving sizzling drops of rain behind.

There was no hurry, and Tiago guaged that they'd moved across the entire city over the last two hours.

Kay finally stopped and removed her gas mask in the quiet foyer of a restaurant, erie in its empty state, though the tables were all set and ready: waiting for the morning crowd. She looked right at Tiago as he removed his mask. He burned his fingers on the wet straps as she said, "I'm turning you over to the warden of the DHC for the bounty. The driver of the prison wagon has been paid to suggest stopping to pick you up."

He felt numb. Outside, Tiago saw through the windows, the rain had fallen to a drizzle. The gaslight streetlamps flickered shadows as the wind flicked their flames this way and that.

"So you do want me back in the hellhole," he said, the misery leaking out into his voice.

Kay pulled out a packet of photos and spread them with a flourish across a nearby table like a card dealer. "No. You'll get picked up, but there's someone inside the wagon that Nashara wants."

Tiago frowned. Kay was helping Nashara why? He couldn't quite put together what was happening here.

Kay leaned close. She was doing it, creating that little bubble of space that seemed to exist just between the two of them. It was some sort of talent, almost magical. "Don't try to figure it out, Tiago. Just take a look at the pictures of the crew of the Zephyr III. One of them will be in the wagon. We need your help."

He looked up and out of the bay windows. He wondered how far he could get if just ran. He had some money, maybe he could stowaway on a boat.

How long could he evade Kay?

Not very long.

She gently grabbed his jaw to point his gaze back down at the table. She'd read his thoughts via his body language. "There's no running, Tiago. Not now."

He swallowed and committed the faces before him to memory, something other than fear building as she put a hand on his back to steady him.

"I'll be there as well," Nashara said from by the door. She'd opened her coat up, and underneath Tiago saw more guns lining the inside than he'd even known a single person could carry. She was a walking arsenal. You rarely saw any guns on the island, too expensive, even for criminals.

"So why don't you just break into the wagon and get the person you want?" Tiago asked.

"Don't want to tip my hand until we know we have the person we want. Otherwise, if we go in too early guns blazing on the wrong wagon, our guy could get hidden further, or put under tougher security. So you're our scout, Tiago. When you give us the go ahead, we move in to recover both of you."

"And if the person isn't there, I get beaten, interrogated, and locked up."

"We will get you out quickly if that happens, we can bribe a few judges, and Nashara is ready to pay you well," Kay said. She was pulling on her poncho. Before she snapped on the bug-like gasmask, she continued. "I have to go meet the wagon. I'll be back shortly."

This was his moment to bolt.

Nashara picked up the pictures of the crew. "Three weeks ago. You remember anything strange happening?"

Tiago stopped thinking about other lives and worlds. "There was a fight. At night. All over the town. Whoever it was burst through walls, fell through roofs. Ripped up road. No one saw much of it. We just saw the damage..."

"It was my grandfather: Pepper was on his way back with information about a new threat to the Xenowealth worlds. He disappeared here, last seen getting aboard the Zephyr III. But the Zephyr was destroyed in a limited yield nuclear blast event nowhere near any of the wormholes out, but a hundred miles north of here in the polar ocean.

"Word is that one survivor from the Zephyr III came back. You're going to help me acquire him. I came with a ship, it's pretty heavily armed up: the Streuner. Pepper didn't have backup, I'm not making the same mistake. Once we're on the ship, it's a run for the wormhole, back into the heart of the Xenowealth, for debriefing."

Acquire him. There was a strange turn of a word, Tiago thought. She was a kindred soul to Kay. Someone who wove the fate of everyone around them.

He was just a pickpocket. It was all he ever really aspired to. His own quiet moments on the seawall, a safe, dry place to sleep. Good food.

Now he was caught up in something that involved the fates of the connected worlds.

"What does Kay get out of it?" Tiago asked, treading into areas which he knew he shouldn't be poking his nose.

Nashara tapped the inside of her coat, and the guns jiggled. "Force multipliers."

"You know what she'll do with all that?"

Nashara nodded, her dreadlocks shaking as she did so. "She plans to run the island."

"She will."

"Maybe. But only if she stops depending brazenly on those modifcations the Nesaru bred into her." She smiled at Tiago's shock that she knew about that rumor. "You're an open book to her. And she holds your strings. But only when she's standing in front of you. She has to learn other ways to get people to do her bidding, and her teachers have been the underbelly of Harbortown. To be a great leader requires more, it requires people to trust you just as much when you're not standing right in front of them. That takes something else. Besides, what she has: it's not that special a talent."

"Do you have it?"

"Yes. Different technology, not biological, but same result. But Tiago, free will's a bitch. Kay can only manipulate. Underneath, we still move our own lives forward. You understand? We fought the entire war over that, back when the Satrapy ruled everything. Before human independence."

Only someone as powerful as she was, Tiago thought, could believe that about free will.

He chose not to say that.

But then, she could probably see him thinking that anyway.

"Here." Nashara pressed a small sliver of metal into his palm. "Jam that under the target's skin, it'll tag him for me and let us know to come get you both."

"Okay." He'd have to keep this out of the cops' hands. Easy enough. He'd snuck small items around the heavy security of The Center.

Outside the loud hiss of a compressed air powered wagon drew closer, and then it stopped. Nashara pulled a large pistol out and aimed it cheerfully at Tiago's head. "Time to turn you in, Tiago."

Tiago had sworn many oaths to never end back up in one of these wagons. Yet here he was again. It was near midnight as they jerked into motion with a belch. Tiago looked around. Unfamiliar, bruised, battered faces regarded him.

For a moment he panicked, not seeing any of the faces from the pictures Kay had shown him. He imagined getting locked away in the sweaty man-made caverns underneath Harbor Town.

Then he saw the youngest face in the wagon and recognized it from the photos he'd been shown of the crew of the Zephyr III. It was just a boy. A boy who was younger than Tiago.

Could he drag him into the net Kay and Nashara had cast?

Yes. The boy was already caught up in the mess from being on the same boat as Nashara's grandfather.

Tiago stood up, tripped, caught himself, and then sat down near the locked rear door.

The boy hadn't even felt the pinprick of Nashara's tiny device.

Tiago waited, tensed, for something, anything, to happen.

The wagon rolled on, turning a corner, headlights revealing ten Ox-men blocking the road with spike strips. The wheels of the wagon exploded as they were shredded, and it rattled to a halt on the rims as prisoners in back were thrown against each other.

Nashara landed on the ground outside. She must have leapt off the top of a building nearby, Tiago realized, as pulverized cobblestone leapt into the air from her impact.

She ripped the door open, shattering the lock, and reached in to pull the boy out. Tiago jumped out next to them.

Three Ox-men ran into the alleyway, eyes wide with fear. "Doacq," one shouted in a low rumble.

Nashara looked down the road. "Tiago, what the hell is that?"

Tiago didn't need to glance a second time. "Oh shit. Shit! The Doacq. We need to get out of here. Now!"

The seven foot tall, hooded figure moved with unnatural quickness down the street. Tiago caught a glimpse, in the flicker of gaslamp, of two large, catlike eyes under the cowl and a slit-like nose.

But it was the mouth that he noticed most. It yawned, the jaw dislocating and stretching like a snake's: a two foot gaping chase of darkness.

The Doacq whipped across the street, slamming into an Ox-man. The jaw dropped even lower, and the Doacq rose taller, somehow, and then the gaping maw descended on the Ox-man.

Hundreds of pounds of rippling, engineered, brute strength disappeared, and the Doacq turned to face the wagon.

"That's a damn wormhole in its mouth," Nashara said, awe in her voice. Then she grabbed the side of the wagon and grunted. "And it's generating an EMP field..."

The Doacq flowed forward, the robe rippling in the slight wind. The massive jaw gaped wider and wider as it got closer. It seemed all maw to Tiago, mesmerized by the black nothingness opening up, propelled by the creature's feet.

Nashara pulled out a large shotgun, and the deafening discharge filled the tiny stone canyon of street and houses. The Doacq twitched to face the incoming shot...and swallowed it all without any change in its approach.

"Son of a bitch," she said, and then leapt forward. The Doacq, ducked and grabbed her, redirecting the energy of the jump to throw her in the side of a house.

Nashara staggered back to her feet in the middle a mess of rubble.

Tiago grabbed the boy and looked around for a place to hide. One of the nearest doors opened, and whip-lean shape of a Runner beckoned at him to get inside.

He needed no encouraging. He ran for the door.

Three explosions shook the street, and Tiago saw with a glance back that Nashara had flicked grenades at the Doacq. It swallowed several, but couldn't be in more than one place at the same time.

Another grenade exploded to its side, and the Doacq faltered.

Shreds of its cloak and flesh splattered on the ground and an animal-like shriek of pain filled the streets.

The Doacq was not supernatural, Tiago thought, dazed. It could be harmed. He paused at the doorway. Maybe Nashara could face it down.

But then the Doacq spotted him, and turned for the building, completely ignoring Nashara.

An Ox-man yanked Tiago into the house and barred the door shut. "This way," the Ox-man grumbled, and shoved the two boys forward through the house.

A trapdoor underneath a table led them under the house, into a hidden basement lit by a single bulb.

"Through here," said a Runner, appearing out of the dark. The shadows made his ribs, visible under a thin shirt, look even more pronounced than normal.

There was heavy, thick steel door a pair of Ox-men had opened. As they passed through that, they groaned shut, and then dropped to the ground as something was kicked out from underneath them. The smell or rank sewage took the breath away from Tiago, and he switched to breathing only out of his mouth.

In the distance, and explosion of brick and screaming startled Tiago. The Doacq must have gotten into the house. With Nashara in pursuit.

They were standing inside a tunnel, lit glancingly by the Runner's flashlight. The center of the tunnel had a wide trench in it, currently dry.

It revealed Kay waiting with a pair of Ox-men armed with RPGs. They aimed the weapons at the thick door behind Tiago.

"So this is our quarry," Kay said, turning on a small penlight to check the boy. "Your name is June, right?"

The shellshocked, beaten boy nodded.

"Can you speak, June?"

"Yes." It was a faint whisper, unsure of itself. But it was the most June had done since this had all started, other than let Tiago drag him around to safety.

"Well June, this is Tiago, and we have to move quickly before the Doacq comes after us. It likes characters like us. It finds us interesting."

Kay led them down the gentle slope of the tunnel at a brisk pace to a junction, where the sound of running water filled the air, and the stench increased.

Five Ox-men stood in a trench full of dirty water holding onto a small metal boat with an electric engine on the back.

Something boomed in the distance, echoing through the sewer tunnels, as they clambered in.

Kay smiled. "That should slow the Doacq down." She waved her hand at the Ox-men and they let go. She gunned the engine up to a brisk whine as the boat shot clear, bouncing off the sides of the trench.

Tiago had a moment to absorb everything now. He turned to Kay. "All this preparation. You knew the Doacq was coming? How?"

"He always comes when there's this much activity," Kay said. "And he's difficult to stop. I thought maybe he was allergic to the sun, but he shrugged off the ultraviolet and full spectrum lamps I installed on his favorite haunts. Since then, it's gotten harder and harder to hunt. I can't even get a good picture of it, cameras fail around it."

Tiago felt like he was looking at a different person. "How can you know so much about the Doacq?" Most of the town didn't even talk about it, they whispered about it and avoided the night. When people disappeared, you didn't dwell on it. You knocked on wood that you would never be the one to turn a corner, and see the Doacq standing there.

"You hunt the Doacq?" Tiago asked.

She heard the stunned disbelief in his voice and turned on him. "It's an alien. It's not some supernatural creature, Tiago. It's like the Nesaru, just more powerful. We don't know where it comes from, but just like the other aliens, it plays on human land as if it owns it. It thinks it rules us, but it doesn't!"

There was a hatred in her face, naked for the two boys to see. She'd let her control slip. "I will destroy it. And then I will take the island. And after that, I will make the Nesaru leave, and the Gahe, and the other stinking aliens that have kept us under their thumb flock through here. Pepper may have failed to kill the Doacq for me, Nashara may fail yet, but I won't."

She turned down another tunnel as Tiago bent over and grabbed his knees. This was insane. They were up against the Doacq?

"You did good, Tiago," Kay said, her face under control again. "You got her to chase you, despite the rain incident. You got her to invest in you, to want to protect you, just enough that instead of grabbing June and running back to her ship, she decided to tackle the Doacq. It was perfect. You have a place among my lieutenants, a place on this island, Tiago. You did well."

He didn't feel like it.

Things had gotten complicated quickly. He hadn't intended the mark to be a living legend.

He certainly hadn't expected to be involved in the betrayal of a living legend.

Tiago shivered.

Kay had a safehouse set up for them. It took getting out of the sewers and back onto the streets, through the alleys and people's homes again. By the time they got inside, Tiago couldn't tell where in Harbor Town he was. They'd doubled back, and around, and it was so late it was now probably officially early. His eyes were scratchy, his movements felt like they were delayed by a half second.

"Don't worry," Kay told him as she took their protective gear. "You'll be safe here. There are people for the Doacq to catch. He'll eventually slow down, turn his attention elsewhere. It's all planned."

It didn't make Tiago feel any better. He caught the eyes of June, and the other boy certainly didn't look reassured either.

But Kay caught that. And she spent time with them until they were mollified, and relaxed. There were Ox-men guarding the house, equipped with heavy machine guns, and escape routes everywhere.

A tall man came in with cold water and sandwiches. Somehow getting something in his stomach took the edge of Tiago's fears.

Maybe it was just having something to do.

"There is more I have to do," Kay said. "The caches of arms Nashara promised me need swept up and stored in secure locations. And eventually, I need to see who won."

She left the room, five foot figure flanked by a pair Ox-men.

June stopped eating. "Do you trust her?" He asked.

Tiago looked up and wanted to say he did, but the words caught in his mouth. "I don't know. She's dangerous to cross."

June gestured at his face. "As dangerous as this?"

"Yes."

"Then I don't want to have anything to do with her," he said. "I've had enough."

The boy looked exhausted.

"I'm sorry," Tiago muttered. "I'm very sorry. I thought you would be going with Nashara."

"The woman?"

"She's looking for someone called Pepper. She says he's her grandfather. She thinks you know..."

"They all do." June looked down at the remains of his sandwich. "He was okay. I liked him. He paid us in gold to get him out of here, but there were ships waiting for us between the wormholes out and the island.

"He fought them off, and then when he realized we were in danger, jumped into the ocean and sank. Didn't stop them from sinking the Zephyr III anyway. They killed everyone but me. Dragged me out of the ocean and took me back, forced me to tell them everything he did, or said."

Tiago wrapped his arms around himself and leaned forward.

The Doacq was hunting them. Nashara may not even be alive, a victim to Kay's machinations, just like Pepper.

And what was he? If she could throw their lives away so easily, what chance did he have of living if he moved closer into Kay's world?

He thought of the contact, the compulsion he had to do what she wanted. It came from her voice, her posture, the way she could read him. And it wasn't real.

With her out of the room, he could struggle away, couldn't he? All that was left was his fear. Fear of consequences.

Fear that she would track him down for betraying her.

"She has a ship, an armed ship, she said, waiting for her. It's called...the Strainer, or something like that," Tiago said in a tumble of words. And then he said something he never would have, had he been doing this for Kay. "If you want, we can try to run for it."

June didn't even pause to think about it. "Yes. I'd run with you."

"I could be trying to trick you," Tiago said.

"I don't care. I'll take the chance. I don't want to be trapped here, I don't want to get eaten by the Doacq."

Tiago found himself nodding with June.

"We leave the moment we see morning," Tiago said.

"So you can spot rain?" It'd be suicidal to try and move through the city without any rain gear. And if he couldn't see the rain coming, he wouldn't know to hide from it.

"Yes. Do you have any family?"

June shook his head. "No. They're dead now."

Tiago did not follow that up with more questions. He didn't want to know.

The Ox-men guarding them checked on them randomly. The moment the door closed, the early sun lighting a band of orange up over the rooftops, Tiago broke the locked windows open. There were other skills he'd picked up in addition to picking pockets.

June started to climb down the side, but Tiago shook his head. "Go up, to the roof. They'll expect us on the street." The Runners and Ox-men would fan out down there, hunting them.

Rooftop to rooftop would keep them out of sight for longer.

Once up there, Tiago oriented himself. They were closer to the docks than he'd dared hope.

They stuck to the roofs, clambering awkwardly up drain spouts and slipping on tiles. But they made it to the edge of the plaza after an exhausting hour.

The docks ran out from the seawall, long piers of concrete stacked with unloaded goods and Ox-men hauling carts back and forth.

It wasn't until they'd walked through the crowds of the plaza, and then up onto the seawall, that Tiago relaxed a little. The Ox-men guarding them would have called the alarm by now, phoned Kay, and the entire town might be crawling with people hunting for them, but they'd at least gotten to the docks.

Tiago stopped a dock worker in greasy coveralls overseeing the unloading of a ship docked almost by the seawall. "We're looking for a ship called Strainer, have you seen it?"

The man frowned. "Streuner? It's over there."

Tiago looked. It was a gun-metal gray boat with a large green flag with a black and yellow X on it.

June yanked Tiago around to face the plaza behind them. The hooded figure of the Doacq stood at the far side, people scattering away from it.

"I don't think it..." Tiago started to say, as the Doacq looked over the top of the crowd right at them, and began to move toward them. "Shit."

"But it doesn't come out in the day," June said, his voice breaking with fear.

138

Kay had said it seemed to choose the night. That her lights replicating daylight hadn't harmed it. He shouldn't have been surprised. But he was. From across the plaza Tiago could see the unnaturally long jaw dislocated and drop, down past the alien's chest, down almost to it's feet. Anything that stood in the way disappeared into it: scared people, tables, chairs. It swallowed them all.

Tiago and June turned and sprinted for the dock leading to Streuner. An act of faith that they could protect them, really, but what else could they do?

They shoved people aside as they ran the slow curve, ignoring the curses aimed in their direction.

When they turned onto the dock and sprinted, Tiago looked over at the seawall. The Doacq barreled along it.

He realized he was screaming as he ran. Dockworkers were turning to look, and then jumping into the water as they realized it was the Doacq.

It gained on them. They had half the dock before they could reach the Streuner, and the Doacq was coming up the dock, may three hundred feet behind them.

Tiago knew he shouldn't look over his shoulder, it slowed him down, but he couldn't help it.

The dark pit of its maw was so wide and inescapable, ready to swallow them, the pier, and anything else.

As to where people ended up when it got them, only those swallowed knew, and they'd never come back to talk.

Tiago realized he was about to find out. He wasn't going to make it to the end of the dock, where the Streuner waited. Maybe even if they made it, they'd still be swallowed up.

Maybe it could eat the whole boat.

He glanced back over his shoulder, and as he did so, a loud boom came from the end of the dock. Something large whipped past his had, and the Doacq staggered and fell.

It's mouth dipped, hitting the concrete of the dock and swallowing a scoop of it, concrete chipping around the edges of its mouth.

Another boom stopped it as it struggled up to its feet again.

Tiago redoubled his run, as did June. He ran so hard it felt like his joints would pop, his brain would be jarred free of his skull, and his lungs would burst into flames.

As they moved clear, the booms turned into an all out barrage. Continuous thunder rolled from the ship, bursting out from large guns that had rolled out of emplacements all over the ship.

His eardrums stopped trying to understand the deafening sound as the entire section of the dock under the Doacq disappeared.

The Doacq had picked the wrong ship to run at.

Two dark-skinned crewmen, just like Nashara, held out their hands at the top of the plank leading on to the deck. Tiago sprinted into them, knocking them over and collapsing, panting, amazed to still be alive.

"Cast off!" Someone yelled, and the plank was tossed free. From his viewpoint on the deck, Tiago saw a tiny rocket shoot up several hundred feet into the sky, dragging a length of parafoil with it.

The foil expanded, filled with air, and the ship began to move.

A pair of feet in familiar boots stopped in front of Tiago's face. He looked up. It was Nashara. She moved slowly, with a slight limp, and wore a patch over one eye. Her hair had been burned off, and one arm was in a sling.

She kneeled and grabbed his hand and said something, but he couldn't hear it through the ringing in his ears because the guns still hadn't stopped: Streuner shivered constantly as it continued firing on the Doacq as they moved away from the dock. Slowly, at first, but then the ship built a bow wave as it sped up.

A few minutes later the entire ship slowly struggled up onto the hydrofoils underneath its hull, and it popped free of the resistance of pushing against water.

They sped away from the docks, the deck tilting alarmingly as the Streuner turned hard toward the open sea.

The alien Doacq was falling further away from Tiago with each minute. So was Kay.

June was still in a room being checked over for injuries, but Tiago was allowed to wander around inside the ship. There were crew cabins, a kitchen, storage rooms, a common sitting area.

Nashara sat there, playing with a small piece of paper. She kept folding it until she had turned it into a tiny flower.

"She sent me to pick your pocket," Tiago confessed, standing at the table. He'd expected the boat to sway more than it did, but the foils kept it almost rock steady. "It was a trap from the beginning. And I'm sorry."

She looked up at him with one eye, and Tiago flinched. What would he do to someone who'd cost him an eye? What would someone as powerful as Kay do?

"I knew it was a trap," Nashara said. "What I wasn't expecting was the Doacq."

"You?" He found that hard to believe, knowing the things Nashara had seen and participated in.

Nashara shook her head. "It's a massive universe, Tiago, with many participants. The Doacq's an important force, and I'm not sure what it's up to. We need to find Pepper, if we can, if he's still alive. If June can help. Maybe together we can find some answers, find out if the Doacq is a threat to us. But Tiago, I'm just tiny player on the edge of some large events. I don't know half of everything. The universe is not tidy. You don't always get quick answers."

It was a sentiment that Tiago felt a kinship to. She felt just like him. Navigating her way through all this just as best she could.

But then that raised his suspicions.

"Are you saying that just to make me feel better?" He asked.

"Do you rule me know, like Kay?"

If she had the same talents, why not?

"I mean, if I'm your pawn, you seem calmer than Kay," he continued. "She isn't just someone organizing street kids, protection setups, scams. Not anymore. Now she's just using us up like our lives don't even mean anything."

Outside the ship slowed, hydrofoils sinking deeper into the water until the hull hit water.

Nashara crushed the little paperbird into a wad. "Sometimes we become the thing we're fighting hardest against," she said thoughtfully. "And Kay is fighting hard against an unimaginable past on Okur. I was there, once. I've seen what she came from. I don't think she will stop fighting it for quite a while."

Tiago thought about Placa del Fuego, caught between the forces of Kay and the Doacq, and wondered if the island would survive the both of them. "She said she'd rule the island."

"And maybe more, no doubt," Nashara said. Then something strange happened, a fluttering sensation in the deepest pit of Tiago's stomach that left him suddenly dizzy. Nashara stood up and grabbed his shoulder. "Come, Tiago, I want to show you something."

She led him out onto the rear deck of the ship, which was dominated by the black nothingness of a wormhole.

Tiago gasped. He'd never seen one this close, towering over his head. Large enough for a whole ship to pass through and that had once floated above a world. Spaceships had once passed through it before being deorbited.

And now him.

The sky overhead was covered by a dark, orange cloud in outer space, whisps of it streaming off toward the horizon. And cutting the sky in half: a silver twinkling band. The Belt of Arkand. He'd heard it mentioned by sailors, and here he stood looking at it with his own eyes.

"You asked if I made you do this," Nashara said. "But this was your own choice. I didn't make you do it. This is your new life now."

But was it the right choice?

He looked around at the strange sea they plowed through, and saw another wormhole far ahead in the distance, propped on floats and bobbing on the surface of the green ocean. That wormhole led to yet another ocean, and more worlds.

More possibilities.

Maybe not the right choice. Only time would tell that. But it was certainly his choice, he knew, leaving all those years of sitting on the sea wall and dreaming behind for a chance just like this.

THE RYDR EXPRESS

You've made your way through the corridors of the train and found your room, up on the third deck. Tea has arrived, delivered by a vaguely humanoid robot that balances its torso on a pair of continuously spinning gyroscopes.

Sitting down at the small table, you let yourself relax just a touch and stir in milk and sugar as the train continues to speed up. Two hundred miles per hour, two-fifty. It has just emerged from a wormhole that led downstream towards even more wormholes that eventually bifurcate. At that junction there are trains to the worlds of Fairwater and Fairhaven.

Outside your window, the purple forestry of Rydr's World whips past. The occasional city slowly accretes around the windows, then fades back away.

Now that the Rydr Express has slipped out of the wormhole at the Western edge of its lone continental landmass it is headed East toward the other wormhole on the far coast. When it hits that wormhole and passes through, it'll start jumping its way toward the Dawn Pillars junction. From there it'll head upstream through hundreds of wormholes, until it ends up in League territory when it exits a final wormhole and arrives on the world of Bifrost.

The Rydr Express is a spur that juts off in that uncertain territory of unaligned worlds that all exist in between the Forty

Eight worlds. They are all connected by thousands of wormholes, and its only been in the last decade that the wormholes have been moved out of space, onto land, and hooked up by rail.

You have nine hundred miles to go before you hit the Eastern coast. Nine hundred miles of tension.

The door to your room slides open.

You drop the spoon to the table. A startling sound: metal on wood. The clattering and reveals that your surprise. It also reveals that you are a bit stunned, and overly nervous.

The tall man you're looking at is wearing a black oilskin coat, and he walks with a slight limp as he slides the door closed behind him.

Inside the small sleeper berth, he dominates the room. His steel-gray eyes flicker, scanning everything, then finish up by pinning you in place. His shoulder-length dreadlocks are graying, slightly, and with the weathered lines of his face, he looks like he's in his forties.

A far cry from the centuries that you know him to be.

You're holding your breath, and the trigger of the gun in your left hip-pocket, where its been all along.

It's a trigger's-width away from releasing hell as the man sits down across from you on the other side of the table. From the creak of the floor underneath, you can tell he weighs double, maybe triple what a man should.

You can't say you weren't expecting this. He's that good. That's what everyone says. But this is your world, your game, and your territory. To have been flushed out before you'd even really sat down is a gut punch.

"This is a private room," you say, mustering indignant outrage. You're still trying to keep the 'traveling businessman' camouflage up.

The man leans forward, his elbows resting on the table and making it creak from the strain. "I'm Pepper," he said, as his locks fell forward and he held out a hand.

You maintain the fiction for another split second, then lean back and retrieve your tea. You're impressed at your steady hand. "Most of my friends," you mutter over a sip, "call me Vee."

"Are you going to pull that trigger, Vee?" Pepper asks, very seriously, your eyes meeting over the lip of the cup.

"I haven't decided yet," you reply, setting the tea down.

Eighteen hours earlier the militia summons jacked you up out of bed with a ringing headache, leaving you stumbling around shaking your head as your partner grumbled and pulled the covers up and fell back asleep.

The klaxon sound, rigged to a bone-induction military earpiece quantumly entangled to HQ, continued on until you patched in and reported that you were on your way, godamnit, and they could quit paging you.

But there was no trip to HQ. Head of operations was standing outside your very door with three other rail agents when you got uniformed up and burst out the door.

"We have a situation," she said.

They all forced their way into your tiny apartment.

"I have some one here," you stammered.

Operations looked over at the door to the bedroom. "Tell them to leave," she said. Then she paused slightly. "How serious is this?"

"What?" You were a bit lost for words. What the hell was going on?

"Your file shows few social attachments. Is this someone we need to take into our protection during this mission? There's a high risk component. An attachment could be a liability."

"Protection," you said, eyes wide. Even if it was only a fling, you hadn't wanted someone's life at risk due to their having the bad luck to stumble into you for a few great encounters.

Operations sighed and pointed at the bedroom door and snapped her fingers. "Make it happen."

One of the agents walked to the door.

Moments later the apartment had been vacated, and the confusion and shouting abated. Everyone'd had a deep breath, and Operations sat in your armchair as if she'd owned it her whole life.

"We have a situation," she said.

"You mentioned."

"Pepper's here on Rydr's World."

"Oh."

"We're constitutionally a neutral zone, Vee. Our economic ties are to the Xenowealth, but we still have two League-loyal worlds downstream of us, and they have peace-brokered rights of transport through us on upstream all the way back to core League territory. We can't have the Xenowealth's top troublemaker running loose. Fairhaven and Fairwater, those worlds are far more militarized than we are."

"What do you want me to do?" You'd been unsure of what all this meant.

Operations clarified that, leaning forward. "Intelligence says he's been around shipping and loading centers. We think he's planning to get weapons aboard a train. Why? We're not sure. But it can't be anything good. We need you to shadow him until he gets out of our territory. Once out, he's not our problem. But whatever he's involved in, we can't have it jeopardizing our neutrality."

You'd licked your lips. "And if he starts causing trouble, what am I supposed to do?"

"Stop him."

"Stop him? This is Pepper. The man is more alien machinery than human. He's more legend than real. I'm probably not going to be able to stop him, Ops, you know that."

She looked at you, and then nodded. "I know that," she'd said. "But we need you to at least try, to demonstrate our seriousness."

And you'd swallowed. Because you realized then that's why they chose you. No family, no attachments.

You're damn good at being a rail agent, there's that too.

But most of all: you're kinda expendable.

And Operations was watching. She'd at least done you the favor of explaining things. They're always honest. It's a volunteer job. Always was.

You could have refused.

But you'd slowly nodded.

Because in the end, how many people ever get a chance to meet a living human legend?

Pepper grins at you, now, as you let go of the gun in the hip holster and put both your hands on the table. "I've haven't really done anything yet, and you're the fair sort," he says. "I like your decision-making process."

"What are you up to here?" you ask.

Pepper leans forward. "How much weaponry do you have access to aboard the train?"

Enough, you hope.

"This is neutral country," you remind him.

He slings an arm over the ledge on the back of the built in seat. "Neutral? The line's swimming with League agents."

"And with Xenowealth agents," you tell him.

He waves a hand, unimpressed. "We just follow the activity."

"Treaties were brokered. Rydr's World seceded from the League ten years ago. But we are also not allied with the Xenowealth. We host trade to both."

"And you let the League run up and down the train lines as they see fit," Pepper said. "That breeds trouble."

"It was a condition of our independence."

"The League knew it couldn't hold onto you, so it grabbed that best possible concessions. You bent over backwards."

You bite your lip. "I'm not here to argue history."

"And yet, it always walks back up the line to bite us all in the ass," Pepper said.

"What are you planning?" You ask him, outright.

"It's not what I'm planning you need to be worried about," he says, and raises a finger.

You both hear the dull thud down the corridor. Your ears have long since been cored out and replaced with synthetics when you agreed to join the rail's security. Yes, you volunteered to defend your planet. Yes you do as part of a self-assembling militia. But that doesn't mean you aren't teched out with the latest and greatest. Quick nerves, reinforced skeleton, subprocessors in the nape of your neck.

A body hits the carpet. A hand smacks the wall. You half stand, but Pepper, expecting something of this sort, shakes his head.

Wait.

The door is kicked open, and Pepper reaches out and grabs the man standing there.

He's a bit stunned. He's holding a large, silenced pistol, but Pepper's grabbed and broken his hand before he's even had time to frown. You notice, in the split second as his entire body is violently yanked from the doorway and over your cup of tea, nudging it slightly with the tip of his boot, that there's blood splattered on the assassin's gloves.

By the time Pepper slams him into the side wall, just under the window, his neck is broken.

Yet, for good measure, Pepper takes the man's own silenced gun, puts the silencer to the dying man's mouth, and pulls the trigger.

Blood and brain tissue spray the window.

Pepper sits back down and delicately pushes your teacup back to its original location on the table. "You were saying something about neutrality, I think," he says.

The dead man will be tied into a battle-net of some sort. You're not wasting time. You're kicking out the paneling underneath your bench seat and reaching under to retrieve a large black case.

Inside, nestled in foam: extra handguns, a tactical assault rifle, ammo, a belt of flash bangs.

"Who are they after?" you ask. "Me or you?"

"They're killing passengers," Pepper says.

You pause. "I can't believe that."

Pepper still has the gun he took off the dead man. He glances around the door. "Follow me and see for yourself."

Outside, in the hallway, blinking at the bright lights, polished brass, steel inserts and other neo-modernist stylings you see the first body. It's an alien: Nesaru. Its quill-like feathers droop from its skin in death. Clear fluids dripped, splashed against the hallway wall, and soaked into the carpet.

The slender, ostrich-like alien's neck is bent in an impossible angle.

"There's more," Pepper whispers.

Each room is a display of death. Different colored fluids. Different bodies. But all punctured, broken, run down. Still. Unmoving. Statues in their nooks, holding gory, distorted death poses for you.

But some of the rooms are empty.

That leaves you puzzled. You're mulling it over, but even as you do that, you enable contact with HQ.

It's quantum entanglement communications. Which means its expensive. Someone has to create the two paired pieces of quantum bits and separate them. You get one bit, HQ gets the other. And once one gets used, and the information passed through, its state reverts to unpaired. It's the universe's most expensive form of limited bandwidth email.

So you telegraph HQ a summary: LEAGUE *KILLING* PSSNGRS. TRAIN HIJACK IMMNT? ADVISE.

Pepper looks inside another empty room, then back at you.

He's expecting you to notice something, but the reply flashes back, painted over your eyesight thanks to a chip in your visual cortex. WCH PSSNGRS?

Which passengers?

And the empty rooms are a puzzle that finally snaps into its proper shape.

You're only seeing dead aliens. There are no humans in here.

NON-HUMAN, you reply.

Pepper's watching your air-typing fingers.

OBSRV & RPRT, you're ordered.

"What do your masters order?" he asks, forcing another door open.

You don't answer. You don't need to. The troubled look on your face tells him everything.

"So what's your plan, here?" you ask. You're keyed up. A little angry. You're also relieved no one has ordered you to detain or try to stop this man.

"Plan?" Pepper looks down the corridor. "To stop it."

"Why?" You do hate yourself for asking, somewhere deep inside. But there is genuine curiosity. What's in it for this man? What is making him tick. "This isn't your fight. This isn't a world that asked you here."

"It's infectious," Pepper says as he points at one of the bodies.

You recoil for a split second, then realize stepping back won't make a difference to survival one way or another. "Biological warfare?"

"No, the violence," he says. He's looking back at you. "It starts here, but then it spreads. Consumes everything around it. Like a fire, it tries to pull in everything within reach. Borders might be decent barriers, but it tries to leap around, continue. So I come out here, to fight it before it has fuel. Before it spreads to the worlds I hold dear."

There's a darting movement, a shadow against the far door leading to the next car. Pepper launches himself forward, boots digging into the carpet hard enough to rip it and make the metal beneath his feet groan as he springs away.

You follow, a breath behind. Fast to the unaided eye, but molasses compared to the snap-speed of Pepper, who hits the steel door and rips it out of its hinges.

He pivots, keeping it to his right side as a shield that smacks into someone you can't see, just as another man bursts down the corridor. This man is dressed in dull gray armor. It's a flowing, shifting exoskeleton that encases him. He looks like a knight with submachine guns in either hand. Pepper drops the door and closes with him.

When he and Pepper hit, it sounds like a padded gong has been struck. Metal colliding with flesh with metal underneath.

Pepper grapples with whining exoskeletal arms, and both men twirl and spin around the corridor, each one looking for a weakness as they grunt, shift, and struggle in their rapid tango.

Still locked together they smash through the door of a cabin.

As the sounds of destruction and splintering walls fill the corridor the ripped off door shifts. A man crawls out into the corridor on his hands and knees.

He leaves a trail of blood behind from his ruined face, where the door struck him as Pepper passed. He has a large gun in one hand, which he awkwardly holds as he pulls himself along.

A new sound creeps out into the train car. Something like the scream of a can being slowly ripped apart, and then a fleshy, wet, thump.

Pepper steps out of the room holding a helmeted head in one hand, torn completely free of a body.

"Pepper!" You shout the name in warning, without thinking about it, and the crawling man raises his gun.

But before he completes the motion Pepper throws his companion's helmeted head at the gun. The shot destroys the dead skull, creating a cloud burst of blood mist that Pepper cuts through to kill the crawling League agent with heel stomp to the back of the neck.

The two of you are alone again.

"I was hoping he'd still be unconscious," Pepper says, looking down at the corpse. "I wanted to talk with him. Find out where the human passengers are being herded too. How many League agents there were."

"And what they were up to?" you suggest.

Pepper shrugs. "That'll emerge." Then he looks up and down the car. "What do you think, up to the front, or back?"

"I can't help you," you remind him.

He looks past you, back down the train. "Are you physically prevented from helping me in any capacity, right this second? Is something literally holding you back? Neural taps?"

You shake your head.

"Then you're full of shit. You're making a philosophical choice. To follow an order. You are choosing to stand by."

Pepper chooses backwards, and you begin to move through the cars door by door. He leads, and you follow.

OBSRV, you think. Yeah. You'll do that. You'll just fucking OBSRV.

Three more cars of death, corpses framed in their rooms, and you catch up. Five League agents ordering humans forward, killing any aliens they manage to catch.

People scream when Pepper kicks the door from the hinges and wades in. But the agents don't. They're expecting him.

They move in synchronization to turn and attack, as if sharing a single brain. Linked to each other in some deep, technologically enabled battle symbiosis. Gunfire rips through the walls as they open up, and you duck back into the space between trains and look through bulletproof glass. The thundering sound of air passing over the rubber, vacuum-proof flexible tube that connects the two cars deafens you, and mutes the sound of battle.

A multi-person ballet of death is ensuing. Pepper sprints into the mix, his trenchcoat flapping around him with each twist and turn. Here he is leaping off the wall, almost hitting the ceiling, to flip around behind the first pair of attackers.

Like Pepper, these five attackers are more than they seem. Wherever the League rose up against the aliens who had once held humanity in its iron grip, they slaughtered former masters and sought to plunder their superior technologies.

Some thought the League was too far diminished, too obsessed with human-only worlds and too pushed back to the fringes. But here are their well funded paladins, and they are faster than you, stronger than you, more vicious than you.

And almost as dangerous as Pepper.

Almost.

One is shot in the back and falls, writhing. Another's head disappears. Was that a shotgun blast? You didn't see one, but it's hard to follow.

Number three's chest is caved in when Pepper runs him through wall, and pulls him back out to use as a shield.

And then the remaining two withdraw, running right past you as Pepper chases them.

A sixth man carrying what looks like a grenade launcher melts out of a room and ghosts past you. He's dressed in a suit, the same camouflage as you, and his eyes flicker sideways as he spots you.

It was a well sprung trap for Pepper. He's focused forward, and here comes the high powered attack from behind.

But this man reads something in you. He isn't going to leave you in his blind spot. He's moving to pull out another weapon with his left hand.

He's faster than you. Stronger, more dangerous.

But he wasn't expecting you, and you have the drop. Simple physics.

Because, much to your astonished satisfaction, you've had

your own firearm out and ready to fire, finger just outside the trigger, since you stopped by the window.

Just in case.

OBSRV!

Forget that crap now. There's only flight or fight now. And flight was kicked in the nuts the moment this man started to twist and reach for his backup weapon, realizing that the damn grenade launcher would kill you both.

You fire from the waist, just out of general principle, as you're bringing the gun up to your trained fire stance. He's hit in the core, which barely registers on him. But once you're up and ready, it's two to the chest and two to the head.

For good measure you empty the clip into his face, revealing metal chips, machine eyes, and more. The man's more metal than human. Which is why you stood over him and kept shooting until there's nothing left.

"Give me the grenade gun," Pepper says, suddenly back in the car. You wordlessly pick it up and throw it over.

He turns around and kneels.

When the door to the car opens, it reveals forty League soldiers, dressed in armor, carrying rifles. Where the hell had they come from?

Pepper fires the grenade launcher through the car, through the open doors, into the mass of soldiers. The doors close. But flame licks around the doors' gaps, the windows bow out, and explosions rock everything.

He walks over and hands it over. "Pick a position, fire on anything that comes through."

"I can't do that," you protest, even as you hold the weapon.

"You already killed a League agent," he says, moving back into the car with survivors. "You've chosen your side. You're in."

He leaves you alone with the grenade launcher, and you reluctantly drop to a single knee.

Congratulations. You're now responsible for a full on, hundred percent, international incident.

Pepper gives the civilians instructions, and returns dragging a large case. "Get dressed, we'll need these to stay on the train."

Inside are spacesuits.

He's right. Whatever the League is planning revolves around hijacking this train. Which means it's not stopping on the East Coast. It's going to dive right through the wormhole leading away from Rydr's World and keep going.

You quickly pull a spacesuit on. It's a transparent baggy film that hangs loosely around you until you press it to the helmet and make a seal. Then the material constricts and sucks itself in to you until it's more of a second skin over your clothes.

All this time you've awkwardly kept the grenade launcher sighted on the far door of the train car.

Pepper looks at you, and a faint flicker of communications laser appears as motes drift through the air between the two of you. That makes sense, you don't want the League hearing you over radio of any type.

"I need that launcher back," Pepper says, and swaps you for a machine gun. "And this is your last chance. To get off the train. If you want."

Get off the train. Return to HQ. And explain you shot a League agent? Covered Pepper with a grenade launcher?

If you were going to go rogue, you might as well see this through.

You've got no soft spot for aliens. Rydr's World was run by Nesaru when your grandparents were your age. You saw the scars on their arms and tattoo barcodes. They told you about forced breeding programs with that aura of shame, but insistence that you know what happened.

There are still Nesaru gated compounds, complete with orbital defenses and full security.

And those aren't going away. Nesaru built those long before

humanity was brought here. They won't give them up, not without a fight that would cost both sides too much.

Awkward compromises had been reached. And time had passed. And Nesaru who worked side by side with humans had always been here, and had helped when humanity revolted and demanded self-determination here, as it did all throughout the known worlds. And for a while, Ryrdr's World was a strong League of Human Affairs supporter.

But when the League began deportation, people refused. It was understandable, leaders argued, but would lead to humans acting like the Nesaru had when they had dominion. Humans would lose Nesaru technical expertise, finance, and technology. The success of Xenowealth worlds, fully integrated alien and human societies, led them to resist purism.

But you know of Nesaru that live in compounds, that despise humans as little better than monkeys. You read their sneering reviews of bumbling human efforts to deorbit wormholes and create a more directly linked system of worlds.

You understand the League, on a fundamental level.

Maybe once you agreed.

Until that single moment, when you walked through the car and saw those dead individuals. Each one, formerly a thinking being. This was the end result of League ideology. If you value one life, think it superior, eventually, taking the other does not matter.

"I'm staying on board," you tell Pepper.

"Good," he says, and behind you something detonates. The next time you glance back through the doors the rest of the train is falling behind, emergency brakes shuddering it all to a stop.

If nothing else, you tell yourself, their lives will have been saved.

The spacesuits' gloves are like gecko feet: they're embedded with pads and microscopic nano-adhesives that allow you to clamber up the outside of the car.

But you're moving along at several hundred miles per hour. It isn't wind you encounter as you crawl up to the roof, but a hurricane.

You're flat to the roof, army crawling along a tremendous, pounding resistance that wants nothing more than to bat you off your perch. The adhesive pads hold.

AGNT: RPRT!

Just barely.

It's an exhausting, sweat-filled haul to get three cars forward from where you were. When you're done, it feels like you climbed up the side of a building.

You dig your pads into the roof and shelter behind the several inches-high protection of a vent and pant.

OBSRVNG HIJACK IN PRGRSS, you tell your superiors. SURVIVORS IN BRAKED TRAIN.

An hour later, the train is still hauling at top speed as it passes through the last stop on Rydr's World. Skyscrapers whip by, and for a while an aircraft paces the train.

You wave at it.

AGNT: RPRT!

You ignore the demands ghosting over your eyeballs.

Fifteen minutes later, you squeeze your eyes shut and feel your stomach lurch as the train hits that blank portal of darkness that is the wormhole leading out and away from Rydr's World.

Pepper shouts. It's joyful.

"Open your eyes, Vee," he says happily, rapping the side of your helmet. "Open your eyes. You never see the full vista from one room window. Not like this."

When you open your eyes the train is whipping past a giant mountain chain. There is no vegetation, and you're deep in the valley. Overhead: the remains of a nebula is scattered over the entire sky. Impossibly jagged peaks rise for miles around you. You feel light.

There is no wind pressure thundering at you.

Five minutes later the train dives into another wormhole.

Right away a giant hand of wind smacks into you.

You open your eyes, and this time the tracks are on a bridge. It stands in the water, pilings driven down maybe ten feet. There is no land anywhere, you feel dizzy looking out at the horizon.

Where the sea laps, smoke wisps and rises. The pilings are burnished and polished, as if the sea is acidic.

Half an hour later you leave that behind. Plunge through yet another wormhole, and when you open your eyes you gasp. You're out in space. There's nothing but the darkness of vacuum and distant stars all around you. Track hangs in space, suspended in nothingness.

You stare at the heavens for twenty minutes, awestruck, until you realize the train is coming to a stop, and that it has been slowing the whole time.

Pepper taps you, and you turn. He points.

A starship approaches. Black paint against the black space all around you. You can see it by the stars it occludes: a darker space slipping over space as it gets closer.

Nav lights and docking lights pop on, and the frame is outlined: a giant functional cylinder strapped to a bell-shaped engine.

"What now?" you ask Pepper.

"Wait and watch," he says.

OBSRV.

The League shuttles thousands of soldiers into the train after they cut in temporary airlocks near the front. Pepper counts ten thousand. That sounds right. They must be literally standing shoulder to shoulder to fit.

And to the front of the train, a sled is being prepared with a rocket attached to it.

"When we last had a full on war between the Xenowealth and the League," Pepper said, "we had a problem. Each wormhole is a natural border. A checkpoint. When they were in space, we stacked orbital firing platforms around the wormhole. Try to shove your ships through, and you'd get hammered. That's how the Satrapy, the aliens, that's how they kept us all in check. But once we had League and Xenowealth, the only way to push against each other was to foment revolution, play secret agent.

"Then, when the wormholes get moved down out of orbit, into oceans, it's the same problem. Natural chokepoints. Then we start running track through them all, thinking of them as just subway stops, that's when the League thinks, ah, now it has a military option.

"But it only gets to use it once."

You're both ready to bet that what's on the sled is a bomb. It rockets through the wormhole ahead and detonates, and then comes the ten minutes later, delivering troops and hardware to secure the wormhole: the chokepoint.

Then comes more.

And more.

"They've probably had this starship mothballed in far orbit ever since wormholes were in orbit here, back in the day, and the League had ships out here, before it withdrew," Pepper mused. "It's not a warship, we've tracked all those and the negotiations made sure those withdrew. But that doesn't mean it isn't useful. They've been smuggling troops one by one to this location for years, staging them in a station that we would have assumed was abandoned. I followed people out here. Followed the activity. Didn't see it being this big."

The League is invading. Not Rydr's World. But the next habitable world upstream of this string of worlds connected by wormholes: Dawn Pillars. A center of trade and activity, a highly developed world. And unlike the polyglot Rydr's, Dawn Pillars has a population that is almost all human. Very few aliens.

Ripe for League take over.

No OBSRV left, really.

You sit down and tap out a report.

There is no answer.

You wonder what that's about. Is you department infiltrated with League? Are they just waiting? Are you that clueless, or ignorant?

Or are they just speechless because you dropped a bomb in their lap?

"What do we do next?" you ask.

Pepper's looking up at the starship. "They hijacked our train, Vee. I'd like to return the favor." He looks over at you. His dreadlocks are floating in the bowl of his helmet, making him look medusa-like. It's slightly disconcerting. "If you don't mind, I'd like to throw you at that ship."

He's not kidding.

Pepper has a half mile of a high-tensile thread, and he unspools several feet of it and ties it off on a tiny buckle on the back of your suit, near the small of your back. Then he throws you over the side of the train, lets you out about six feet, and starts spinning you around over his head like you're a bucket on the end of some string.

The world cartwheels around you, and then stops as Pepper lets go, the timing impeccable. He's slingshot you toward the dark bulk of the starship.

You fly through space, falling in, and then Pepper slows you down, using the brake on his spool.

After you reach out with your pads and grab the hull you look back and wave.

The thread yanks at you as Pepper activates a motor on the spool. Two minutes later he lands next to you, you both glance around, and then begin crawling around the hull of the ship.

The way in presents itself: a manual emergency airlock near a set of bay doors. You move to undog the first hatch to cycle in, but Pepper stops you.

"Not yet," he says. "Not until they finish unloading."

An hour later you both make your move. The manual airlock deposits you inside a cavernous cylindrical hanger. You scurry across the curved walls, weightless, using your gecko-fingers to grab any surface you can and then kick off.

"Keep up." Pepper moves like a cat in the air, loose-limbed and graceful. A natural hunter. And he knows what he's hunting. He's taking you to the core of the ship.

You suddenly get the feeling this isn't the first time he's done this.

He has a silenced gun out, and everyone you cross in the corridors of the ship ends up spinning slowly in the air, a surprised look on their face, blood slowly drifting out of punctures in the forehead.

Swift, quiet, calm, suddenly violent.

And fast. You're pushing off every bulkhead as fast as you can to keep up. You've bored down through most of this ship's bulk in minutes.

The men guarding the cockpit barely have time to register the fluttering trenchcoat, the man spinning in the air and firing, dreadlocks spread out around his face.

He's through them and into the actual cockpit of the ship in the blink of an eye, and shouts of outrage end with the silent thwack of Pepper's response.

"Shove them out and lock us in," Pepper orders. He's floating around from control pod to control pod, his head cocked, as if getting advice from someone. Maybe he has quantum entangled communications of his own. Someone's talking him through what the controls are, you think. Someone deep in the heart of the Xenowealth.

Screens flicker on, and you hear the wail of wind outside the door.

Glancing at the screens showed you what just happened: the ship vented its air. Airlock doors throughout are wide open to space, and you can see up on the screens random faces, tortured, blood beginning to leak out of orifices.

You look away.

"Any of them good about drills and who kept near their spacesuits will be trying to get back in here," Pepper said. "So stay clear of the door, they might blow it."

He's listening to instructions and moving quickly from place to place, frowning.

Then the engines thunder to life, and he claps his hands.

"Oh, they're not going to like this."

There are no weapons systems on this ship. It's transport, pure and simple. Which is how the League was able to leave it behind, hidden away from Xenowealth and Rydr's World military negotiation accountants looking for just this sort of stunt when comparing inventories and current ship names and movements out of the area when Rydr's World demanded independence.

But that doesn't mean it can't be used as a crude missile. Pepper orders you into a acceleration pod to strap in, but keeps spinning around and flitting around to control the ship.

You're not moving fast when you strike the train and track. But its fast enough to rip the outer hull of the ship and derail the train. It's fast enough to twist and rip track.

The impact throws Pepper around the cockpit, his body smashing equipment. He wearily pulls himself out and gets back to the controls, firing the engines to pull the ship free of the track and turn it about.

The ship's external monitors, shown on screens all throughout the orb of the cockpit, show cars full of soldiers and equipment hanging around the ship. The staging area is chaos.

Pepper lines the ship up and fires it up. It shudders and caroms its way down the tracks. It speeds up, heading for the wormhole leading to Dawn Pillars.

"Pepper?" you ask. "What are you doing? This thing can't go through a wormhole."

"These ships used to do it all the time," Pepper said.

"Yes, when the wormholes were in orbit. Now they're deorbited. We're going to drive this thing through that hole and out into a train station that's on a planet's surface."

"I know."

There was, you could hear, a sort of boyish satisfaction in the tone of Pepper's voice.

When you pass through, there was that familiar kick in the gut. And the sudden resumption of gravity, yanking down on you again.

And then it all turns bad. The walls flexing and bending visibly. The creaking superstructure that then began to give up creaking and just start screaming.

There was what felt like a mile of sliding, and tumbling, and then darkness as the energy systems on the ship all failed.

Someone is chuckling in the background of the debris and shaking and...yes, that's an explosion somewhere nearby crackling the air.

The next kick isn't in your gut, but to your helmet, which cracks and falls away. And then you pass out.

A lot of men make a point of arresting you when you wake up in quiet, very clean and modern feeling hospital wing. They've vacated other patients and have what looks like a small military guarding you.

No one is happy.

Very grave people are making very important, and measured, but Very Serious accusations. People wearing very expensive suits who look perpetually constipated.

No one is sure what, exactly, to charge you with, but ramming a spaceship through a wormhole into an urban world has repercussions, they explain.

You ask about Pepper, but they pretend not to hear you.

On the second day, when you're able to get up and walk, you stand by the window and look out over the city. And you see the wormhole and the central train station. And you note the long furrow in the parks and space around the wormhole made by the massive spaceship, the ruined hulk of which rests at the end of the giant, debris-scattered, ploughed mess it has created.

You helped do that.

No wonder they're pissed. At least four buildings have been subject to a rapid and unscheduled demolition by spaceship.

You're going away for a long, long time.

But was it worth it?

You hear mutters from some of the soldiers guarding you that the League managed to overwhelm a couple of worlds this way. There's fighting with the Xenowealth breaking out. It's the League's last stand. And they're going for broke.

Which means that even if you helped delay them, those surviving soldiers, even without the benefit of surprise, are still going to try to shove through that wormhole any minute now.

You've been stripped of your volunteer rail militia communications equipment by a surgeon who cuts out the implants. A formal letter declaring you persona-non-grata has arrived. You're stripped of rank, pay, and your pension has been scuttled.

That is your afternoon. The Rydr's World embassy liaison has you sign here, there, and here, and here again to formalize it.

They will not be helping you find legal counsel in the upcoming fun.

But after the glowering liaison leaves, one of the guards taps your shoulder. "Legal's here for you," he says, and points out a room.

Inside is Pepper, dressed in a suit, holding a briefcase.

As the door closes behind you, he sets the case down and opens it. "So, I'm here as a Xenowealth ambassador," he tells you. Inside are citizenship ID chips, a few wads of hard currency and some gold coins, and several wads of explosives.

You don't bother to ask how he got all that up here.

"You can't follow me directly anymore," Pepper says. He motions for you take everything but the explosives. "But these chips are a new identity anywhere in the Xenowealth, and starter cash. Go on a vacation. Start a business. But just one favor, Vee?"

"Yes?"

He's shoving the explosive into the wall, careful to point the shaped charges in the needed direction. "Don't ever work for someone who demands you stand still and do nothing."

"I can do that."

"If you're not interested in a vacation, call the person on that card. Tell her I recommended you. She'll know what that means."

You nod.

Pepper walks over, pushes you behind him, and blows the wall off the side of the hospital. "Apparently," he shouted, "even the diplomats can't get these guys to let you go, so I have to get involved. I hate administriva like this, but I wasn't about to leave you pay the price for my little joyride."

He's holding out his hand. You're not sure what the hell comes next, but you stop near the edge and look out over the city, the wormhole, the train tracks, and the destroyed ship, and then take a deep breath and jump with him into the air.

Five adrenaline-fueled hours later, you're on a train by yourself, wired, jittery, and feeling the kick to the gut as your train indolently passes through a wormhole on its way deep into the Xenowealth.

You flip the plastic business card Pepper gave you around.

Nashara, it says. And there's the contact info.

So there's the question. Do nothing? Take the starter cash. Settle in somewhere. Start a business? You can do anything.

Or make the contact.

What will you do?

RATCATCHER

Pepper's vision fades slowly away in the empty midnight as he tumbles end over end. His eyes frost over, moisture crackling and icing over pupils, hardening against his eyelids. The pinpoint stars fracture behind the fractal cold of the ice, then shatter into a multitude of glittering refractions.

Unseeing, he still stares wide-eyed into the vacuum.

A wisp of his last breath congeals in the top of his throat, a half-swallowed spiky sponge of air that clings to his tongue. Two grinding cracks thunderclap in each eardrum, and then there is silence.

The prickling sensation on the inside of his skin has faded. Before that, he endured the pain of fluids being sucked out through his pores. For a while he could feel the cold in his bones, but even that has gone dead.

He is dead.

Dead and coasting through the vacuum in the lonely dark.

Drifting.

There's enough still working under the skin and muscle to register the impact. Pepper comes alive and grasps for a handhold, slides over pitted metal, then catches something. He can't tell what it is. He has a half second of strength and awareness to spend. A half second upon which so much depends. He's investing the precious spark of energy in priming mechanical triggers to force a frozen arm awkwardly into motion.

He blinks. A scraping, cornea-scratching shaving of ice shatters and floats away.

He's hit the airlock. That was the goal, though it feels like something he decided a century ago. Time is dilated, dialed down.

There's a cloud of flaking skin, blood, and spit, all of it turned into ice and drifting around him. Pepper pulls himself to it and raises a fist. Strikes it once. Twice.

And that's all he has.

Electricity jolts him back awake, back arching as hearts suddenly kick online with a surge of adrenaline released from artificial glands. Pepper vomits blood. He can feel it seeping out of his pores and starts to raise a hand.

Something slices deep into his wrists. He stops.

Blind and deaf, Pepper retreats. Focuses down until he can feel the presence of footsteps just out of reach.

Then there's the problem of the nano-filament wrapped around his wrists. It winds its way around his arms, up his chest, around his neck, down his back and bound his legs together. The slightest motion will cut him apart into a hundred different slices.

Unexpected. This had definitely not been part of the plan.

As his eardrum flimsily heals the damage, Pepper listens to the calm breathing from the other person in the room. "I need something to eat," he croaks.

The tiny machines buried in his bloodstream have been knitting him back together. But they need fuel. They are stripping it from his body's metabolism, which has fed them all the non-essential tissue it could already. Now he can feel the fever chewing through muscle.

"I'm sorry," says a voice. High, possibly female, with a faint tremor. "I'm watching you heal, watching your body eat itself. All that meat's got you back alive, but that's about it. You're weak, now. And that is the way I prefer you."

Pepper's vision is back. A little cloudy, perhaps, but functional. The floor is a functional self-cleaning industrial plastic. A nearby first class leather recliner is mounted to the floor, and a pair of functional hiking boots shift slightly.

She taps a spot just in front of her ear. "De Fournier, confirm. All available resources to the Hakken Depot of Line Three-Zero-B. Cross check with D. Franklin, case manager, for authorization and budget allocations. Suspect hostile."

"How about water?" Pepper wiggles slightly. The nano filament digs deeper into skin on his back from the motion. But he is able to look up above the boots.

"Do I look that naive to you?" the owner of the boots asks, looking down at him. The compact woman's face has been aged by sun, weathered by time. She leaves her straight hair gray. The crow's feet at the corners of her eyes tighten as she smiles sadly down at Pepper. Her brown arms are covered in New Anegada tattoos, Teotl-style serpents wrapping both her forearms outside her bullet-proof vest.

She's pointing a high calibre gun at his temple, but keeps herself at a respectable distance.

"Yamaxtli de Fournier," Pepper says. "You are anything but naive."

"I've been tracking you for five months," Yamaxtli says. She pulls a small, black notebook out of a shoulder pocket on her vest. Flips through the pages and stops. "The whole story is in here."

She turns the open notebook toward him. Pepper can see the faded pencil strokes of carefully written Nahuatl. She taps a line. "Yes," Pepper says. "I remember that."

Yamaxtli's lips narrow with disapproval. "I don't, no thanks to you. I got up this morning and the last good memory I had was twenty years old. Not a happy one, but not a bad one. A fight with my daughter. But I knew something was wrong with it right away: it felt so distant. The haziness everywhere. And then I look down, and on my arm in henna is a note to myself to read my notebook.

"It's an old habit I had, even before the damage to my brain. When working the case, I keep a narrative. I wrote down what I did, how I came to conclusions. It was the story of my investigation. Apparently, after the neural damage and before my memory implant, I kept the book to help myself live week to week instead of day to day. Thanks to this old wound." Yamaxtli taps a faint dent on her forehead.

"A bullet to the temple, and yet you stayed on until you helped them catch her," Pepper says. He looks around the train car. They're definitely in first class. It's also been totally cleared out.

No bystanders. Yamaxtli is thorough.

The stars twinkle outside the windows. The train is whipping through tracks out in the gulf of vacuum between two wormholes. Pepper finds himself missing the comfort of the small spaceship he'd jumped out of to get here. At the time it had seemed cramped, barely big enough for just him and his supplies as he lurked out there in the dark, waiting for the signal to leave it.

"According to the crib notes of the story of my life, I've been back to work and had quite a successful twenty years. They call me the Ratcatcher. Retrograde amnesia only took a year out of my life. Once I had my neural implant installed and successfully synced up, I could keep memories again. Until you, seemingly deliberately, destroyed my ability to keep memories when I tried to bring you in." She runs a finger over a burn mark just under her right ear.

Pepper is overriding cramping muscles, sending relaxants down his bloodstreams to handle the fact that he is hogtied by nano filament and unable to even breathe too hard. "Really?"

"Says here, ever since I started tracing you, others on the case have mysteriously dropped away. No one has shut the case down: that would have gotten noticed. But people kept getting offers to leave for better departments. Others sudden had family problems. Someone even won an off-planet lottery."

"Lucky for them," Pepper observes.

"I cut communications," Yamaxtli says. "Went dumb with technology. Which is good, because even after you took my memories, the case was all right here for me on the paper. You were trying to knock me out, Pepper, without outright killing me. Which would have been noticeable. But it didn't work."

Pepper would nod, if the action didn't slice his neck. "You are more dangerous than most people might imagine."

"I'm not dangerous," Yamaxtli says. "I don't kill people. I *catch* people who kill people. Like you."

"Fair enough," Pepper says. How much time does he have to get out of the filament? He's thinking about strategies. He's not going to be able to talk her out of this. And if he does something really stupid, he might have to hurt her. "What happens next?"

Fucking filament. Where did she get that from? He hadn't known she had it.

"Now I'm back up on communications," Yamaxtli says. "You didn't smash that ability, thankfully. I called for backup to take you in at the next stop."

"I heard you send up the beacon," Pepper says. He had hoped she'd stay dark, give him time to convince her to get him out of the filament before the shit hit the fan.

Instead, he is going to have to improvise something.

The wormhole's maw is just minutes away. To Yamaxtli, Pepper knows it doesn't seem like more than a few minutes before the train hits it. Then there'll be a faint flip in their stomachs. Darkness. Then the train tracks burst out somewhere else.

They might burst out onto tracks running on barges that bob next to a floating city. Or maybe they'll be on a coast. Perhaps the other side of that wormhole will see them trundling through the center of a hollowed out asteroid.

In some places the tracks will be out in space again, but hanging over a planet or swinging around some strange sun. The Xenowealth has pulled more and more of the entire wormhole network closer together to run tracks through them. The trains ferry increasing numbers of citizens around every day. The tracks connect planet to planet through wormholes. It takes just hours for a high speed train to cross from world to world.

In theory it's just minutes before the train starts to slow down to pass through the wormhole, and then to stop at a station where people with weapons will swarm the car. Yamaxtli isn't relaxing, but she certainly thinks the end is in sight.

But things are really only just beginning, aren't they?

"I have a theory," Yamaxtli shifts her weight. The gun in her thin hands looks oversized, almost comically large. But she holds it steady and with familiarity. The holster on her left leg is rubbed smooth from use and age.

"Tell me," Pepper says. He's only half paying attention. He is more focused on cranking up his senses to reach further out. To listen for any faint sound or any motion that isn't quite right. He's been slowly trying to ease the nano-filament around his wrists back down his forearm. If he needs to, he can now slice his hands off at the wrists to gain motion from the elbows forward.

Blood trickles down the small of his back off his arms from the motion as nano-filament tightens and digs in further.

"These implants, the changes to your body. You've remade yourself from the core out. I don't think you're human anymore, Pepper," Yamaxtli says. "I think you've been gone so long, seen so much blood, fought in so many wars, you have no perspective. And now that the Xenowealth is no longer fighting revolution, now that we're using economy, research, negotiation, to slowly pull over the League, what is there left for you? These planets, these peoples, there was a time you were desperately needed in the war against our enslavers. But in peace, you became so used to killing that you started searching out chaos and death: it's your

173

programming. Your reason for being. All those little chips in you, it's all they know to do. And you found the way to continue on… as a serial killer."

Pepper rolls his eyes. "You say that so confidently I could almost believe you," he says. "But you know it's bullshit your expert 'researchers' fed you to make sense of the data."

Yamaxtli's expression doesn't change. "You think I'm unsure?"

"Until I hit you with an EMP to disable your brain backup you had a memory implant to deal with your retrograde amnesia from that bullet to the brain. You have new eyes. Bone grafts for the osteoporosis. Glands to stimulate muscle growth. How does it feel to walk around without that extra motorized help in your right hip? I noticed you have a bit of a limp. Does that make you less human, or just aging?"

Yamaxtli nods. "You argue that it's all degrees?"

"Pacemaker… or backup heart. It's very gray," Pepper says. "I for one have just followed the idea that I should be all that I could be."

"But what are you being?"

Another rivulet of blood splatters to the floor as Pepper shifts filament by shoving it through skin. "You don't really think I'm the Line Killer," he tells her. "You have doubts."

There is a faint discomfort in her face. But Yamaxtli smiles sadly. "Doesn't matter what I think. I'm the Ratcatcher. I bring you in. The researchers, the judges, they'll do their bit. They'll study you, study the evidence, and we'll find out what is true."

She has her doubts. It's written across age lines and the crinkles in the corner of her eye. But she's a professional. She's got sixty years of hunting under her belt and she's damn good.

She's the Ratcatcher.

"Politically, this has to be complicated," Pepper observes. "You are brave to have taken it on. Or it is a strange form of career suicide."

The uncertain look in Yamaxtli's eyes disappear. "Yes.

Franklin thinks that. Give the old woman an impossible task: catch one of the founders of the Xenowealth: a killing machine that made our enemies nervous and destroyed our oppressors. Accuse him of being a serial killer."

A smile flicks across her lips. Pepper returns it. "I'll bet they didn't anticipate that call you just made."

"It's inconvenient, having the founding fathers still around," she says. "Much like the younger supervisors in my department might wish the old Ratcatcher wasn't around to correct them and suggest improvements as they muck up basic security work. Maybe some people would prefer you faded away and stopped popping up."

There it is. A shiver runs through the train. She notices it as well, but doesn't take her eyes off him. Sharp. She taps an earpiece. Nothing. It'll be dead.

Yamaxtli, for the first time, looks somewhat unsure. "What's going on?"

"The train is stopping," Pepper says. "The real killer has arrived."

Without the acceleration their cars reorient. The mild feeling of gravity gives way to weightlessness. Pepper shifts to catch blood that has pooled around his lower back, soaking it up so it doesn't float away. He's been shoving nano-filament around, letting it slide under his flesh and carve muscle in order to get it bundled up where he wants it. The skin and muscle has healed, but at a cost: energy burned from consuming even more muscle.

He is emaciated now. His clothes hang like rags on him. But even that is giving him room to shift more nano-filament around that had been looped around a different shape.

Yamaxtli kicks off a luxurious designer-leather chair to the nearest doors. She forces them to slide open.

As Pepper had suspected, there are no other passengers in the other train car. Yamaxtli buffered them to protect civilians.

The train shivers, and then an explosion further on down toward the engine reverberates through the cars a second later.

"Who?" Yamaxtli asks.

"Your killer is an Individualist. It's name is a unique encryption key, but I call it Vlad."

Yamaxtli stares at him from the doorway. "Bullshit."

"I do indeed call it Vlad. The thing is really into impalement and some other creepy shit. You read your own your notes, you saw all that fucked up shit about flaying. You have to know it isn't really my style."

Another shiver from up near the front of the train. Pepper imagines Vlad is going through the train cars one by one. He hopes Yamaxtli has cleared the *entire* train of people using her authority, but looking at her paling face, he can tell that each explosion and shiver means lives.

"I was tracking the killer as well," Pepper said. "That's why I kept showing up. Always minutes behind."

"But why is it coming at us now? How?"

"It knows you have me. It knows I'm weak, if you are reporting my capture. And for Vlad, I'm one of the bigger trophies around the Xenowealth. It's tried to snare me. We've tumbled. I get away. Study it."

Yamaxtli is barely keeping an eye on Pepper now. It's all eyes on the car ahead. "The Individualists, an alien society older than ours and more advanced, crossed thousands of lightyears and a great war to get to this quiet zone of wormholes and survive... just to commit serial murder?"

"Serial killers exist no matter what civilization looks like. Why not Individualists? You thought I was capable of it. Why not an Individualist?"

She pulls her notebook out and scribbles notes in.

"Let me go," Pepper says. "Unleash me." This has gone too far. He needs to figure out how to protect her.

"No," Yamaxtli says, though she's uncertain.

"Listen," Pepper says quickly. "What's something you would never tell anyone?"

Yamaxtli ignores him and pushes off into the other train car. She pulls a bag along with her, letting items trail out of it as she moves. Thumb-sized impact drones, flash bang mines, directional EMP emplacements, more high-calibre handguns.

"I'm not letting you go," she says. "But I do think you are telling the truth that trouble is coming down the train at us."

She's sticking defenses on walls and strategic surfaces. But it's mostly non-lethal shit, aimed at disabling the sort of tough, human trouble that is most definitely not what is moving from car to car toward them.

It is time for this to end. Time to get them free of this. "What is something you would never tell another soul, ever?" he yells again at Yamaxtli.

She glances back at him, frowning.

The door to the car is ripped off its hinges.

Flash bangs light up the car's interior, wild chaotic shadows dancing across the walls and the starry windows. Concussion charges thud. It's loud and disorienting, but not to Pepper. His eyes adjust to see the shape of the Individualist silhouetted against the spitting sparks left by the dying defenses. The Individualists were a conglomeration of various species struggling to survive against a greater threat. Most of them opted for caterpillar-like body forms: hundreds of manipulators and half-biological, half-machine carapaces.

Vlad isn't like other Individualists. Vlad takes takes being an Indivdualist seriously and is its own shape: bipedal. The biological armor exoskeleton it has instead of skin is bone-white and serrated, covered in spikes and maleficent swoops.

Yamaxtli fires into the maelstrom of light at the one persistent shadow, reloading one-handed via magazines floating in a careful line over her knee. Her back is to the nearby bulkhead so that each shot doesn't propel her backwards in the lack of gravity.

Fall back, Pepper urges. Run.

But Yamaxtli won't. Not even as the massive heft of bone and spikes launches itself casually across the car at her, ignoring the bullet strikes for the tiny swats of annoyance they are.

The impact drones dart out from behind the sumptuous first class chairs and slap into it. The air ripples. Pepper feels electromagnetic pulses dampen the electronic world.

"Shit," Yamaxtli says.

Vlad looms, continuing forward.

Pepper finally gets the worst of the nano-filament free with a last, skin-slicing, peeling shrug that leaves muscle bare to the air and streamlets of blood expanding out around him into a cloud of light red mist. He doesn't have mass anymore, he is no more than a skeletal vision of what he used to be.

But he still has speed.

And armfuls of nano-filament.

Pepper loses his right hand to pull away the last of the nano-filament, then uses it as counterweight. He tosses nano filament in spinning configurations gyrating all through the room in various patterns. A shield and an attack at once.

But Vlad, in a sudden burst of speed that seems impossible given the eight foot tall size, weaves, ducks, and spins away from the nanofilament. Yamaxtli keeps firing throughout all this. She throws more drones at it, but it keeps coming.

There is a split millisecond. Pepper makes the decision.

"Let her go, she's a civilian," he shouts.

"The hell I am," Yamaxtli snaps.

And then it is over. Vlad has redirected and spun the nano-filament around them with all the skill of a bony spider. It pulls back. "You are both prey and that is all," it says, speaking for the first time. "Trophies. You are both mine."

It jerks the net forward and Yamaxtli screams as the filament bites into flesh. Vlad doesn't seem to mind the trail of blood hanging in the air as it pulls them back through the cars. Just gently enough not to slice them all up… just yet.

Pepper grabs Yamaxtli and spins to put his back to the filament, grimacing as it sinks in. "It'll dig into my skin, but not past my bone," he says.

She doesn't protest this. She curls up slightly as her back keeps bleeding. "You stayed. You should have run."

Pepper looks around at their crude, wobbly cage and then down at his missing hand. "I was not expecting the nanofilament," he says.

They fall silent as Vlad pulls them through cars further down the long train. Cars that had been full of living people just minutes ago. They now float in rows, hammered to the luggage racks over their heads by long nails of bone run through their chests. Bubbles of blood grow from the white bone spikes.

Yamaxtli stares at the bodies.

One of them twitches and moves, then groans.

The alien carefully guides them into a large, clear sack. It holds onto Yamaxtli for a moment, pulling out a jellyfish-like device that fastens to her scalp. She hisses and struggles, then goes limp as the tentacles latch on. Blue light pulses, then the alien pulls it away and seals them both in.

Yamaxtli jerks back to consciousness as Vlad pushes open a door. There is no more train in front. Just a mangled mess of metal on the track that used to be the engine. "What did it just do to me?" she asks, voice shaking slightly.

Air whips out with them as they burst into space.

"It scanned your mind for malware," Pepper says.

"You too? It was horrible."

"Not me. We tried that once. The Individualists know better now." He is hardly paying attention to her, though. He's looking through the sack toward the glint they are hurtling at.

"Zero gravity," Yamaxtli muses with a sudden half-startled laugh. "It's comfortable. My doctor suggested that I might prefer moving somewhere lighter. Now I'm cursing myself for not retiring. People tell me: you've lived such a long life. Well, I still have a lot to see and do. This is a shitty way to end a long career."

Pepper has stopped paying attention. He's looking at the smooth cylindrical object moving towards them.

"There it is," he whispers. "A rare bird."

An Individualist ship. One of only five that snuck through into the Xenowealth before they'd managed to shut the wormholes down.

Pepper has always wanted one.

Vlad the Individualist pulls them down a corridor of horrors. There are creatures, intelligent or not Pepper can't tell, frozen in moments of fear and mounted to the walls. A beetle-like alien rearing back from a door, legs out in some kind of defensive pose. A ten-foot tall hummingbird with fluorescent wings yanked apart into constituent parts, each one framed like some anatomy illustration, looms over a room as they pass by. Pepper glimpses more figures in the shadows.

And the human section. Varnished skulls decorate the bulkheads, teeth wide and grinning into the murk. Full humans, naked, are posed with arms outstretched in a freakshow of an honor guard that they pass below.

There is a throne room deep in the heart of the cylinder. The walls are all bone. The throne itself is covered in flayed skin from a multitude of species.

"What's something you'd never tell another person?" Pepper asks. Yamaxtli jumps. They've been quiet for the whole trip down into the throne room of the ship, watching each new contorted body slip out of the dark air toward them, then fade away. "Something so secret, that if I could tell it to you right now, you would know it was a signal from your past self that you could trust me implicitly. Think about that secret, hold it in your head, and I'm going to whisper a single word to you."

Yamaxtli is staring at Pepper, the horror outside the transparent sack they're in forgotten. She looks old, vulnerable, and for the first time, scared.

Pepper leans forward and whispers a word into her ear. A word that only she could know the significance of.

She begins to shake. "No."

"You were a child. The elders told you about the old ways. You couldn't have stopped them."

Tears hang in the air. "So I once told you why I became the Ratcatcher, and now I cannot remember," she said sadly. "Why? What purpose…" She is, Pepper knows, thinking about seeing a clearing in a park near the edge of a town, deep in the heart of New Anegada. Leaving with the respected elders, chanting the old words in the old ways. The comfort of tradition.

Only this time it's different. They are meeting far from the lights of town.

Yamaxtli's bright, young eyes would have not understood the first few seconds she saw the person tied to the stone at the center. But when the obsidian knife came out and struck ribcage, when the still-beating heart was ripped out from under flesh. And her parents stepped forward toward the blood.

Old school religion, Pepper thinks. It's dead now. But Yamaxtli saw it practiced before she could even write.

In the here and now, he sees a quick understanding rushing into her eyes as she moves past reflection, memory, childhood horror, into realizing what this meant. If she has told Pepper this, something she would never have told anyone else, it means she had trusted him at some point and told him and then *never written it down*.

Pepper nods. "Eat your notebook," he says.

"That is *everything* to me."

"This was your idea," he says. "Trust yourself."

"You could have tortured that memory out of me…" she starts to say, but Pepper rolls his eyes. Her hands shaking, Yamaxtli nods and pulls her notebook out. Even under torture, she would never have given out *that*. A secret so dark, so buried.

The sound of a ripping page seems to fill the entire universe, but the Individualist is moving around its throne room, tapping at consoles. It pays no attention. The ship is shuddering, moving away from the train tracks.

"Keep eating," Pepper urges in a low, measured tone.

Yamaxtli rips page after page, grimacing. "It tastes nasty. What is this?" A tiny wisp of smoke leaks from around the corners of her mouth. "It's burning me."

"This is all your idea," Pepper whispers. He's keeping himself between Vlad and Yamaxtli, blocking the line of sight. "Keep eating."

Vlad twists around, suddenly curious.

"Keep eating," Pepper hisses.

The alien whips toward them. The clawed fingers rip into the filament, ignoring the shards of bone that slice off as it rips a wide hole open. "What are you doing?" it asks, the voice powerful enough to shake Pepper's chest. "What is this?"

It flings Pepper aside. He bounces off a wall of bone. There are alarms, alien in cacophony but recognizable in their urgency, coming from around them. It fishes Yamaxtli out of the net, knocking the notebook aside as she tries to eat one more page.

"What are you trying to hide from me?" it demands. "What is this?"

It grabs the notebook, and drops it just as quickly.

Smoke roils out of Yamaxtli's mouth, nose, leaks out from her eyes, and congeals in the air between the spiked, ivory alien and her mouth. Shields of translucent energy rip up out of the floor, seizing Pepper in an invisible fist. Yamaxtli, hovering in the air as well, gasps. More smoke billows from her pores as she's squeezed.

"I am not the hunter," Vlad says slowly to Yamaxtli. Then the Individualist looks over at Pepper. There is a battle going on under the bone-white spikes. Something shivering inside of it as its insides are torn apart. "You are not the hunter."

The smoke is fading. Yamaxtli coughs and clutches her sides.

"This... frail thing. This is the hunter."

"And you," Yamaxtli spits black bile and goo as she struggles to speak. "You are the prey."

Vlad the Individualist slumps in the air. The spikes crumble, disintegrating into a fine ash that hang in the air. The rest of the bio-armor collapses away. Hanging in the air is a three foot long, pale slug, neural implant tendrils tangled in the air.

Yamaxtli attacks it with a pen, stabbing it until fluids mix with the ash in the air and trail around them in wet, ropy strands.

The invisible fist still refuses to let Pepper go. He twists in place to better see Yamaxtli.

"Your idea," he says.

"My idea," she repeats, voice hoarse. "We were hunting the same killer."

"Yes. You realized it couldn't be done alone. You were a little harsh on yourself. You said I should be the bait, and you the Trojan Horse."

Yamaxtli vomits more black bile. Coughs. "The pages."

"Let them run their course. A two part weapon. One half in the pages, the other in a virus present in your saliva. It will pass." Pepper twists around, looking at the bone-clad walls. "The nano-filament, where the hell did that come from?"

"Black market weapons fabricator," she says. "What now, Pepper? We're trapped."

"There's company coming," Pepper twists back to her. "Just hold on."

Yamaxtli coughs again. This time it isn't black bile. It's blood. "I don't think there's much more to hold onto."

"You hang on," Pepper repeats. "Yamaxtli?"

Her eyes close. Blood hangs in the air around her mouth.

Pepper yanks harder against the force holding him. Magnetic fields, gripping any and all metal in him. Maybe even down to the iron in his blood. He pushes, what little raggedy muscle he has left popping and straining. His veins seem to remain in place, but there is a grating sound on the bone as implants scrape.

The new arm and leg he replaced after visiting Chilo have a lot of ferrous material. They'll both stay put. Implants, nodes, assorted machinery, that'll all stay as well.

Messy human remains? All that should be able to move.

Pepper strains. Tearing sounds move to audible. A pop, a crack, and he begins to pull at his right elbow. The joint rips apart. The tearing of skin comes, starting where the bone has punctured the elbow. The pain comes and goes, the regulators are themselves being torn out as Pepper continues to grunt.

His left knee buckles and shatters. Pepper helps it along, digging the fingers of his left hand deep under the skin and pulling.

Implants pierce through the skin and muscle as Pepper finally rips his biological body into the air in a cloud of blood and viscera. He sees himself in the reflection of a mirrored surface: skeletal, missing an arm and a leg, clothes thick with dried and new blood. He was as much a horror as anything else on the ship.

"I made you a promise: that you would drag that murdering fuck back to New Anegada," Pepper wraps his good arm around her waist and braces against a chest of ribs under his boots with his one good leg. "Now hold on tight, this is going to hurt."

Yamaxtli is not breathing, and does not respond. Pepper starts to rip her free of the fields, pulling her free of the pins and implants that came naturally with old age in the developed Xenowealth. As they rip away from her papery skin he winces.

He drags her along with him toward the corridor.

Back through the hall of terrors.

Back to the airlock.

It takes far too long to figure out what an alien manual override looks like. But when he does, the air blows out of the lock instantly.

The temperature begins to drop.

Pepper fastens himself to the wall by looping his good arm

through a ladder. As the blood soaking his clothes begins to ice over and stiffen, he looks at Yamaxtli. She is peaceful, wedged near the crack. And ice cold, his eyes tell him.

As for him, what little flesh that is left on his bones sizzles. There is almost nothing left. He is the walking skeleton that is death, sitting here to guard Yamaxtli against Death.

Pepper laughs.

Soon come, Yamaxtli. Soon come.

It has been three weeks since an interplanetary train was attacked by an Individualist. Three weeks since agents swarmed the Hakken Depot and waited. And waited.

In the old quarter of Capitol City, deep in the Dread Council's citadel, alarms sound. The alert goes out: Individualist ship inbound. The planet of New Anegada kicks into high alert. Ships thunder down out of orbit to provide cover on the incoming wormhole a mile outside the harbor.

And still they are unable to do anything as the long cylinder flashes out of the wormhole along the tracks, ignoring everyone as it speeds for Capitol City. It speeds past Parliament, past the citadel and shrugs off the anti-aircraft fire, and it settles right down at the Depot where all train lines connected in the heart of Capitol City.

Agents inside the Rail Agency rush to look out broken windows as the Individualist ship hovers just a foot over the old marble flagstones. Seconds later, Ragamuffin ships still glowing hot from orbital reentry circle overhead to surround it.

The bottom of the ship disgorges Yamaxtli de Fournier and the frozen remains of what is left of the Individualist. Pepper watches from the corner of the ship's bay as she walks toward the Rail Agency. Yamaxtli's new eyes gleam silver and her arms are now ribboned with matte black swirls that cut through her tattoos.

She drags the body of Vlad behind her in a large clear sack as Rail Agents stare at her. On the steps to the lobby, she stops in front of someone Pepper assumes is her supervisor. He zooms in, sees the name patch: D. Franklin.

Franklin stares at her. "We thought you were dead," he says after a too-long moment.

"I was," Yamaxtli says. "But I'm doing much better now."

Franklin isn't sure what to say to that. "That doesn't look like Pepper," he finally says, looking at the corpse.

"Pepper sends his regards," Yamaxtli says. "But he isn't the killer. This thing is."

Franklin looks down at the bag of organic sludge. "Really?"

She hands him a chip. "All the info is on there. You had me tracking wrong. Follow the info, and we'll be dumping a bunch of evidence out of the ship in a few minutes for you to pore over."

"What about you?" Franklin asks.

"First, I'm owed a favor by the people who are flying that ship around. So I'm going to have them take me to all the horrible vacation spots I've always wanted to see throughout the Xenowealth. And after that, I think I'll consider a new job offer."

Franklin hasn't been expecting that. Now that he's faced with suddenly losing her, he understands what he'll lose in the department. "What will you do?" he asks miserably.

"We're going to hunt Individualists," Yamaxtli says happily.

Franklin makes a face. "What makes you think you can do that?"

Yamaxtli points to the corpse by his feet. "You're standing on one I already caught. The serial killer was an Individualist."

Franklin jumps back in surprise.

As she walks back, Pepper gives the command. The bay vomits bones and humans in stasis, the remains of the many numerous species kept as art aboard the ship. They'll be poring over all this for months.

Pepper moves back into the shadows until the doors seal shut.

"I thought I'd feel more," Yamaxtli says. "I've been a Rail Agent for as long as I can remember. Moving up and down the line, catching criminals that hop from planet to planet and jurisdiction to jurisdiction. I'm neither happy nor sad."

"It's going to take a while for the neural connections to your new memory to link up. Another month," Pepper says gently.

"I know." They'd both been in healing tanks for weeks after Pepper's contacts reached them.

"In the meantime…" Pepper reaches into a pocket and pulls out a brand new notebook and a pencil. Yamaxtli takes them, flipping through the paper and smiling as her fingers riffle through. "Record some new memories."

Yamaxtli nods. A whole blank page to explore.

"There's the whole Xenowealth out there," Pepper says.

It is time to go see it.

HOW THE XENOWEALTH CAME TO BE

Like many artistic endeavors, how I came up with the Xenowealth is probably half personal myths and misremembered anecdotes that I tell myself.

One of the earliest seeds of the Xenowealth probably comes from a very early novel I started writing in high school. It was about an invasion of Earth, one in which not only were humans outmatched but put under colonial rule. As someone growing up on an island, the colonial history and post-colonial history of the region could be found everywhere I turned. I wanted to try and capture some of that history of what it would be like to be overwhelmed as an entire people. I want to write about what it would be like to cast off and find your own destiny, even with your own mistakes along the way.

One of the striking images that I carried with me during that period was of a massive starship, remnant of a large colonial empire, rusting away in a tropical harbor. An image that I still have yet to deploy, but it is a consistent power cord that I return to whenever I come back to the Xenowealth.

That novel was destroyed in the hurricane of 1995 that forced my move to the United States, but in college I kept circling back to some of what I remembered about the canvas.

Several early, unpublished short stories of mine feature brief brush strokes of the Xenowealth. A name of a planet. The attempt to fuse the Caribbean and space adventure. But the spark that ignited the Xenowealth as we know it was a character named Pepper.

My junior year of college I was in a college writing workshop where I wrote a story set in what I viewed as the moment before some colonial empire brushed everything away and squatted on Earth. I created Pepper, a character that broke things as much as he fixed them. This was the story called *The Fish Merchant*.

And it worked. It was one of my first short story sales.

In 2000 I took on a senior research project. I wrote four short stories around a common setting, and the setting was the Xenowealth. I spent six months researching wormholes, building a map, naming planets, and creating a broad canvas hundreds of years further into Pepper's future. None of the stories were publishable, but the Xenowealth firmed up in my head.

When I was first asked to submit a proposal for a novel in 2001, I sketched out the world of Nanagada, lost to the Xenowealth but an important part of it. And I slung Pepper far into the future.

Alas, Crystal Rain did not get a nibble at first. But I took the ideas I'd created out for a spin in a story called *Necahual*. Set in the furious time after New Anegada (Nanagada) is reconnected, it shows the League of Human Affairs trying to reconnect it during their attempt to rule the Forty Eight Worlds. Necahual is, if you read it closely, somewhat non-canonical. I'd place the time line between the novels Ragamuffin and Sly Mongoose.

Nalo Hopkinson took *Necahual* for the amazing anthology *So Long Been Dreaming: Tales of Postcolonial Science Fiction* in 2004.

When I was writing my first novel, *Crystal Rain*, I spent a great deal of time on the world of New Anegada, and a lot of time hinting at the wider world. And fans who'd read *The Fish Merchant* knew there was a wider universe. But other than the senior research project, it was never really super fleshed out until I wrote my second novel, *Ragamuffin*.

Writing a sequel was the most challenging thing I'd done to that point. *Ragamuffin* required me to commit to the implied universe out beyond, and it required lots of hard decisions. I rewrote the first third of that book many times. There are more words discarded off the page of Ragamuffin than on it. But it was during those two years of grief and rewrites that I figured out the Xenowealth and its history.

I also began to flesh out Pepper's history and began to realize that I was going to have to explain how he came from Earth of the near future to Nanagada of the far future.

So I wrote a story called *Manumission* that took Pepper from the time of *The Fish Merchant* into the occupation of Earth where I found a reason for him to go into orbit. That story came out in *Baen's Universe* in 2008, just before the third Xenowealth novel, *Sly Mongoose*.

A story called *Resistance* also came out just a few months later in a John Joseph Adams anthology called *Seeds of Change*. This story showed Pepper working for hire on a space station, again in the context of an occupied solar system. But this was an intimate piece that stayed just inside the station and didn't address much of the Xenowealth.

The novel *Sly Mongoose* was a delight for me to write as I finally got to name the Xenowealth. In my mind, the canvas I'd created for all these books was post *Sly Mongoose*. I was just trying to catch everyone up.

I was gearing up in late 2008 to begin writing the fourth Xenowealth novel, tentatively titled *Duppy Conqueror*. My plans were to show the detente between the developing Xenowealth and the League. I wanted to really have fun with the idea of a wormhole system, and figure out where the Xenowealth I'd created went.

Alas, it looked not to be. My editor and I ended up realizing that it would be better for my career to pause the Xenowealth novels and move in a different direction. It was tough to leave a world I'd lived in for eight years. I took the chapters I had of *Duppy Conqueror* and fashioned them into a short story for the July 2009 issue of *Clarkesworld Magazine* called *Placa del Fuego*, reasoning that at least Xenowealth readers would have that story.

For a couple of years I figured that was that.

Thankfully, I was very wrong.

In 2011, spurred on by seeing writers successfully using Kickstarter and seeing opportunity, I launched a Kickstarter for *The Apocalypse Ocean* (formerly *Duppy Conqueror*). It funded, and I got to write the entire novel. Much like *Ragamuffin* I had to commit to more world building about the Xenowealth. The manner in which human beings were forcibly genetically manipulated into new shapes and forms, the damage done that continues for generations as a result of subjugation, all of this was stuff I'd been wanting to explore. The Xenowealth might be high octane adventure, but those themes about colonialism I'd been wanting to explore ever since the initial image of the rusting starship in high school were ever at the back of my head.

While I was writing *The Apocalypse Ocean* I was approached to write a story for the anthology *The New Heros II*. That allowed me to show hints of where the Xenowealth was headed: connecting wormholes with trains. The League getting more desperate. Pepper becoming more bloody. *The Rydr Express* is probably, for now, one of the closest things fans will have to the fifth novel.

The latest story written before this Kickstarter went back in time to continue moving Pepper closer to the events of the novels. *A Cold Heart* was written in 2014 for Neil Clarke's *Upgraded* anthology. After a couple of years away from Pepper, it was like slipping into a well-loved old trench-coat to be back with Pepper in a short story. It was that story that got me thinking about collecting the Xenowealth stories into a single collection.

It is fascinating to me that the Xenowealth is read by graduate students via *Necahual* in *So Long Been Dreaming* and by gaming fans in *The New Heros II*, and also by online readers in *Clarkesworld*. It has been such a wide place to inhabit. It has shown up scattered across so many contexts.

It is a strange thing to look back on 14 years of a place that once lived only in my head and is now jigsawed together across a series of books and stories. I didn't plan all this. A smarter author would have written all the stories and purposefully connected them to get readers more excited. I wrote these here and there, as chances came to me. As strong ideas begged to be written.

The Xenowealth, in much the same way, has evolved in fits and starts with me. From me drawing spaceships lying in the water in the tropics, to me trying to reframe history by telling readers the story was set on a far-off world in a far-off future.

I do know this, though: realizing how few stories I've actually written in the Xenowealth has prompted me to make sure that I do more of them in the future.

The tales of the Xenowealth are far from being finished. There are many more characters, and worlds, still floating around in the hazy mist that has been developing around all this.

Pepper has many more foes to vanquish.

ABOUT THE AUTHOR

Born in the Caribbean, Tobias S. Buckell is a New York Times Bestselling author. His novels and over 50 stories have been translated into 18 languages. He has been nominated for the Hugo, Nebula, and John W. Campbell Award for Best New Science Fiction Author. He currently lives in Ohio.

SIGN UP TO HEAR MORE

If you enjoyed this book, please consider joining the newsletter at www.TobiasBuckell.com. Updates are only sent out when new books or stories are available for you to read, and no more than once a month.

Made in the USA
Charleston, SC
13 November 2015